The SleepWorker

The SleepWorker

CYRILLE MARTINEZ

TRANSLATED BY JOSEPH PATRICK STANCIL

Coach House Books | Toronto

English translation copyright © Joseph Patrick Stancil, 2014
original French edition © Libella, 2011
originally published in French in 2011 as *Deux jeunes artistes au chômage* by Libella

first English edition

Liberté • Égalité • Fraternité
RÉPUBLIQUE FRANÇAISE

This book has been supported by the French Ministry of Foreign Affairs as part of the translation grant program. Cet ouvrage est soutenu au titre des programmes d'aide à la publication du Ministère des Affaires étrangères.

Cet ouvrage a bénéficié du soutien des Programmes d'aide à la publication de l'Institut français.

LIBRARY AND ARCHIVES CANADA CATALOGUING IN PUBLICATION
Martinez, Cyrille, 1972-
[Deux jeunes artistes au chômage. English]
    The sleepworker / Cyrille Martinez ; translated by Joseph Patrick Stancil. -- First English Edition.

Translation of: Deux jeunes artistes au chômage.
Issued in print and electronic formats.
ISBN 978-1-55245-302-5 (pbk.).
    I. Stancil, Joseph Patrick, translator II. Title. III. Title: Deux jeunes artistes au chômage. English.

PQ2713.A79D4913 2014   843'.92   C2014-905320-7

The Sleepworker is available as an ebook: ISBN 978 1 77056 399 5

Purchase of the print version of this book entitles you to a free digital copy. To claim your ebook of this title, please email sales@chbooks.com with proof of purchase or visit chbooks.com/ digital. (Coach House Books reserves the right to terminate the free digital download offer at any time.)

1

The name New York New York comes from New which means new, newish, novel, from York which means York, and from New York which means New York.

For some time now, the city of New York New York has been home to a growing number of writers, many of whom are well known. Recent studies tend to suggest that these writers owe a part of their fame to the fact that they live in New York New York. By virtue of the fact that living in New York New York would be an asset for anyone aspiring to make a name for himself in literature.

It must be noted that writers from New York New York may or may not write books that take place in New York New York, that talk or don't talk about New York New York, but, in any case, seem to gain from having been written in New York New York. In return, the writers of New York New York don't write so much about New York New York as much as in favour of New York New York, or for the sake of New York New York.

As brief as they might be, the biographies of local writers never forget to mention this: 'lives and works in New York New York.'

As for foreign writers, about whom a word must be said: whatever their country, region, town, rare are those who have never mentioned the city. The name New York New York has this quality of being adaptable to any language, any dialect, any accent. It's been the object of translation in just about all of the living languages.

In any case, New York New York was the first city to propose a Writers' Quarter.

Not simply a quarter of café backrooms squatted in by writers. Not a quarter where publishers have set up and invited writers to come visit. No, the expression *Writers' Quarter* was to be taken literally. In New York New York, there was a quarter where the entire population was made up of writers.

All it took was a single writer to one day decide to physically establish himself there and to set his bestselling novels there for the other New York New York writers to say to themselves, That's where it's all happening now, let's go settle in this cheap neighbourhood that's good for writing, where it's possible to be a bestselling author.

So it was advertised that New York New York offered a residential quarter particularly welcoming to writers. The news spread in writers' circles, and gradually little niches started to appear, writers' niches here and there, scattered over a mixed area - novelistic moments and poetic brilliance interspersed between zones of literary desert.

Of course, they were only minuscule niches at first. If a writer happened upon a colleague while walking on the street or doing his shopping, the encounters were still quite rare. They'd say it was due to good luck when the two writers liked each other, or bad luck when they couldn't stand each other.

And, to say the least, writers flocked, from the verb *to flock.*

Writers flocked there to the extent that non-writers very quickly began to no longer feel at home. The new neighbours were hardly willing to say hello when they'd run into each other in the communal parts of buildings. Let's be clear, if writers came to live in the Quarter, it was to be among writers, not to talk about the weather with the first non-writer who came along. Now, to try and engage in conversation with the writers, the non-writers of the Quarter couldn't find anything better to talk about than the weather. To which the writers didn't respond, or else they did so monosyllabically, grumbling, in order to make their interlocutors understand that these meteorological questions were of no interest to the literature of today.

Writers and non-writers of the Quarter didn't have much to say to each other, only Hello, Good evening, maybe Thank you when one held open the door to facilitate the passage of the other. Most of the time, the two parties communicated with each other via a simple batting of eyelashes signifying It's fine, Don't worry, I get you, asshole.

In the name of a gathering of literary forces, or in other words, in the name of creating a hub of literary excellence, writers benefited from various minor perks: special menus in restaurants, buy-one-get-one-free beers, special rates at the movies, line cutting in theatres, being served first in stores, more services in the library, discounts at bookstores and record stores, reserved parking spots, priority in getting a spot at daycare, a free man with every rental of a woman, tolerance regarding public intoxication, a blind eye turned to the possession and use of drugs.

At stores, overcharging non-writers compensated for the lack of earnings. Non-writers paid more so that writers paid less. Unheard of, thought the non-writers, who came together in associations to complain about this preferential treatment granted to literary workers. In the end, the verdict came down that, as a hub of literary excellence, the Writers' Quarter of New York New York should follow its own rules, exceptional rules, rules that no one was supposed to ignore. In other words, submit to them or get the hell out.

Disgusted, the non-writers gave up the fight. Non-writer tenants terminated their leases, which were turned into writers' leases. Non-writer owners sold their apartments to writers eager to invest their royalties in real estate. The non-writers exiled themselves to neighbourhoods where life would be sweeter, where they'd be taxed less, neighbourhoods where they could attend to occupations other than literary ones, where they could go on about the return of the good weather if they so fancied without it getting them blacklisted. And for god's sake, they wouldn't be bothered with writers and literature ever the fuck again.

Once the quarter was emptied of its last non-writers, a zoning regulation was instituted, with fiscal incentives to rent to confirmed writers.

Real estate agencies specializing in writers' residences put new criteria into place for access to housing. A request could be submitted under the conditions that the writer could prove publication of a book by a legitimate publisher, with a print run of more than 2,000 copies, and that his/her editor and/or agent be the joint guarantor(s).

Anyone who had never published a book had to give up living in the quarter. Anyone wishing to make a name for himself in literature had to get an address there. At first glance, it could seem expensive, real estate agents admitted during their showings, but you'll see, it'll be worth it in the end. What you pay today, you'll get back tomorrow, first in symbolic capital, then in royalties.

The only non-writers of the quarter were clerks working in stores for writers, bankers in banks for writers, real estate agents working in agencies for writers, and all the providers of services appreciated by writers: home deliveries, technical assistance, housekeepers in maids' costumes (or the nudist version), escort services and other commodities. Which goes to show the number of industries that, indirectly, fed on literature.

Mornings and afternoons, the writers wrote in their writers' offices. At noon, they went out to lunch in little writers' restaurants where they could choose from express lunch menus. In the evening, they met for a drink, or, let's say, a drink to start off with, a drink that led to many others, and that's how they got started on a bar crawl of all the coolest places. Later, those who hadn't crashed yet made up noisy tables at semi-gourmet restaurants, before ending up at nightclubs where only the well-known writers could get in. Finally, the most resilient finished off in extremely private clubs with dim lighting and they left feeling relieved or just plain shitty.

Saturday mornings, the writers bumped into each other at stores specializing in household supplies and the nutrition of the literary class, where they'd taken up the habit of doing their weekly shopping. Saturday afternoons were dedicated to cultural activities, so the writers went to museums, galleries or the movies before sending out invitations to go over to each other's houses, with the chance to devote themselves to one of those drinking binges that lasted until they were exhausted, out of words or sick as dogs. Sunday, if it was nice out, the writers organized giant picnics in the park. If it was lousy out, they preferred to hang around at home, lazy blobs that could stretch a sweatsuit out of shape, not moving from the sofa except to go pee, alternating naps and TV, too lazy to wash – it's not pleasant to see a writer the morning after a party in winter. Luckily, spring and summer were livelier. The writers rented buses and went to the country or the seaside for a few relaxing days, extended weekends that they called 'conferences,' 'seminars' or 'study days.'

Outside of this perimeter, New York New York didn't account for any more writers. At least, not officially.

Originally, it was planned that the Writers' Quarter would ignore the question of genres in literature. Among the writers, everything could be found from novelists to poets and playwrights, as well as non-novelists, non-poets and non-playwrights. But in fact, the applications of some New York New York poets meeting the criteria for publication and circulation imposed by the real estate agencies were systematically rejected. Apartments were granted to better applications than theirs: novelists with over 5,000 copies in print, novelists with over 8,000 copies in print and novelists with more than 10,000 copies in print. No poet managed to live in the Writers' Quarter, not even by sharing an apartment with a novelist friend. Same for playwrights and for non-poets-non-novelists-non-playwrights.

Poets and non-novelists were reduced to living scattered around the rest of the city, among the non-writers. This resulted in making them difficult to locate and contributed to their lack of visibility in the literary sphere. Why would anyone waste their fucking time combing through the area, just to take inventory of a few dozen or hundred non-novelists? A Writers' Quarter had been created, and from there things were simple: anyone who had an address there was a writer, anyone who didn't have one was a non-writer.

Some promoters, sensitive to contemporary poetry's lack of visibility, offered to remedy the situation by establishing a Poets' Quarter. They wrote up a proposal, put it forward to the city, which responded Why not? and appointed an independent evaluation committee composed of two writers, a sound poet, a critic, a journalist-critic, a teacher-critic, a professor-writer, a bookseller, a library curator, a lexicographer, a reviewer and a director of cultural development. Under the presidency of a highly renowned poet, the commission examined the proposal and at the end of six months issued an expert report, which came down to the following:

Aside from the development of a housing-residence park intended for poets whose professionalism has already been proven via publication by legitimate publishers, we don't really understand how the creation of a Poets' Quarter will promote an active symbiosis between the inhabitants and literary creation while allowing for the authors' own writing projects. Public meet-and-greets with the author and his books? Literary impact of proposed actions? Territorial anchorage? Insurance of revenues in the medium term? All these elements were overlooked. If you add that the subsidies allocated to journals are very insufficient relative to their importance in the poetic field, we are permitted to doubt that this proposal has correctly taken the measure of poets' needs and expectations. We can ask ourselves if, in place of encouraging a new dynamic, such a quarter risks isolating poetry in a space that no one will enter and that no one will leave. A ghetto, no thank you.

We hear you, retorted the promoters (offended) – if that's how you see it then too bad, we'll cancel the project. But don't you go complaining later. You'll be the first to blame when you go broke.

As of that day, the poets ceased to be considered a category of writers. They were poets, period. They were representatives of a distant era, prestigious all right, but it was obvious they had a hard time adjusting to today's realities. Poets were well liked, but that was it. It wasn't unpleasant to have to use the notions of poetry and poetics from time to time: that being said, it was possible to use them and still do without poets and their books with fewer than 2,000 readers – after all, a novel can be poetic, and a novelist possesses a poet's soul as well. In New York New York, like elsewhere, there were enough great dead poets to not have to give a shit about the few living ones.

People began to speak about poets in the past tense. It was said they had disappeared. Having reached the end of a race, they had become extinct. They'd lived their lives, they'd had their history, a beautiful and tragic history, subject matter perfect for a novel. Now it was better for them to just vanish, leave the prestige of past poetry intact and spread its legend to future generations, rather than endure long and sad death throes. Better to die a poet than to live as a writer with fewer than 2,000 copies in print.

And New York New York could present itself as a poet-less land, a great novelists' city.

Less than a year after its creation, the Writers' Quarter had become *the* hip place to be: the place in New York New York where it was cool to be seen hanging out, where it was desirable to have an address.

Any author of a bestselling novel had a duty to live in the quarter. Anyone wishing to find housing in the quarter was required to write a novel and get it published. Novel production felt the effects. Tons of new novels were printed. They arrived en masse at bookstores, which no longer had room for a Poetry or Non-Novel Non-Poetry section. The Newly Released Novels section took up the entire sales floor.

It was the time of the novelists, the young novelists. They always had something to say. Always a comment in store, a witty remark ready to let fly. Guiding them was their need to express themselves and make that known. They said they had a special thing called World Vision. Which often led them to have visions, and always concerned the world in its globality. Each new World Vision was tested out in conversations at bars, in restaurants, in public debates, in local media. And, depending on the reception that each received, they'd decide whether or not to write a book about it. A film or at least a screenplay? They would rely on their insight to formulate a personal and sensitive vision of the world in which we are condemned to live, you see, so we might as well accept it and just read the novels of today. In private, they gladly opened up about their pride at having succeeded before turning thirty. It was a habit of theirs to intransitively use the verb *succeed*. They'd managed to turn a manuscript into a bestseller, so, in a nutshell, they'd succeeded (unlike others). Obsessed with this powerful sense of accomplishment, they'd acquired the certainty that they embodied the literature of their time. Their critic friends recognized in them a talent for capturing the vibe of their era, a capacity to describe transformations of the present and envision paths for the future. The first book was a youthful impulse, the second a transition toward the third, which was the work of a maturity that following works strove to consolidate into one sensitive and singular oeuvre.

Under the pretext that they were the most important voices of their generation (one only needed to see how much they were both quoted and solicited), they claimed and secured housing in the quarter. Each time an old novelist died, his apartment was taken over by a new bestselling novelist. By virtue of which, the Writers' Quarter became theirs.

Since novel production didn't stop growing in New York New York, since everyone wanted to do the young-novelist thing as new novelists popped up every day, and since each new novelist exercised his right to housing, the Writers' Quarter became saturated. There wasn't a single apartment available, not even a cellar or a tiny room to sublet. Even if you were an established writer (with more than ten books officially published, including paperback editions, translations, adaptations, reviews, quotations, exegeses, congresses, conferences, symposiums, prizes, grants, residencies), you would be told: sorry, we don't have anything at this time, the demand exceeds the supply, too much literature, not enough housing.

Rents skyrocketed. The Writers' Quarter became completely unaffordable, among the most expensive neighbourhoods in the city. It got to the point that living in the Writers' Quarter became inaccessible to the majority of them. The writers who'd been there from the beginning, its founders in a way, the first writers to inhabit the quarter, were also the first to leave it. They sold their writers' lofts to guys from television, to actors, journalists and other finance types who had moved on to writing novels. After settling down in the Writers' Quarter, guys from television, actors, finance types and journalists persisted in the writing and publishing of books. They said: We're the writers now. We know the formula for a bestseller. It was a smash hit in bookstores.

2

The future parents of John and of Andy have this in common: they aren't native New Yorker New Yorkers. It's what they became. From godforsaken places in the middle of nowhere where they were starving and bingeing on films, they applied for naturalization. Within a few weeks, they'd gathered the necessary pieces to compile their dossiers, completed the appropriate forms, appended their signatures to the official documents and addressed the whole thing To Whom It May Concern. After reviewing their cases, the Commission for the Study of Migratory Flow summoned them to undergo a medical examination, as well as to enlighten the authorities about their motivations and political convictions and to inform them of their skills and professional qualities that could benefit the city. Finally, one hand over their hearts, the other raised with the palm open, they swore they would settle in the big city with, certainly, the goal of living there, but above all, to work there.

It was the glorious era when the arrival of migrants still gave rise to public ceremony. The goal was to welcome you and to wow you. On that day, it was nice out like summertime – it wasn't actually summer, but it was just like it. The weather was nice, hot, conducive to a general euphoria. A system of heat-producing streetlights by Scialytic covered the public space with the lighting of an operation table, eliminating any shadows and generating an artificial warmth.

Everything was hot, everything was illuminated. No shadowy areas, no dark streets, no way to escape the reign of the all-illuminated.

Crime, which as we all know likes to do its dirty work in the shadows, was to take a hit.

Maximal lighting, security for all. Now that's a slogan.

So, on this first day, with a feeling of maximum security, the migrants celebrated their arrival to the city. They were invited to parade around on decorated floats typical of public revelry – it was like being at a carnival or a parade celebrating the homecoming of military or sports heroes. Except not. The heroes of the day were the new arrivals.

In front of the floats, a freelance actor bustled about. For a fee (the amount of which would forever remain confidential), it was his duty to set the mood. An operation that came down to three points: 1) chanting into a megaphone, 2) encouraging the passengers to repeat in unison, 3) waving at people.

Strange waving, intransitive waving. But what human could receive these waves, and if need be, respond, since the city was empty, given it was Sunday and its inhabitants had stayed home to watch the game or left for the weekend to get some fresh air? Empty city, no one on the streets, no one in the buildings, miles of deserted sidewalks, a spectacle without spectators, and everyone on these floats waving their hands.

What is the meaning of this ceremony? How can these gestures be interpreted? Why all the waving? What good does waving do when there's no one to see you wave?

Nevertheless, even with insanity looming on this hot afternoon, John's and Andy's future parents executed their waving with an enthusiasm worth mentioning. They were waving for the sake of waving. Because it was part of the protocol. Because these waves carried with them an inaugural force that it was proper to deploy before living in this great city. And, to accompany their waving, they blew kisses.

Positioned along the route, loudspeakers set the tempo of the party. It was a party with a lot of bass. A party without bass isn't really a party anymore. There's something missing: the bass is missing. The sound of full-on bass is good for slapping you with a migraine. For that matter, Mr. Andy, a man prone to the slightest little pains (which he will die of) couldn't escape it. He endured the consequences of these boom-booms that make for the best migraines, which is unfortunate because the day was turning out to be very, very long.

The hours came and went without the slightest sign of exhaustion from the freelance performers. Still so much bass and waving to generate. The parade dragged on. Enough is enough, for god's sake, let's get this over with, John's future parents complained. We're not going to go down all of the streets and all of the avenues, are we? Andy's parents chimed in (as fate would have it, the two couples were occupying neighbouring spots). Can't we just finish this parade, go home, and have some peace and quiet? all four said in unison.

For a long time, they awaited a signal. Nightfall, for example, or a drop in luminous intensity – something to indicate the late hour and the beginning of the end. Alas, nothing came to slow down the parade or disrupt the protocol. Night didn't fall.

Or rather, under the effect of the Scialytic lamps, the night was lit up, and the moon and the stars were shoved behind a vault of artificial light.

At the end of twenty-four hours of non-stop parading, the floats dropped the families off one by one at their assigned housing.

I'm beat! sighed Mrs. John, plopping on the couch.

I've had it! exclaimed Mrs. Andy, wondering if it was worth it to shampoo her hair.

Finally home! Mr. John let out, cracking open a beer.

I need a pill or I'll die! Mr. Andy shouted, opening the medicine cabinet.

At these words, without a fuss, John's and Andy's future parents crawled into bed, closed their eyes and crashed.

And, no later than the next morning, each of them went to work.

Like their new compatriots, John's and Andy's future parents dived into New York New York books, watched New York New York movies, listened to New York New York music, went around to museums and galleries in order to see art from New York New York.

If they wanted to treat themselves to a book, their first priority was to purchase a book written by a New York New York writer. If they had to buy a CD, book a concert ticket or choose a film at the cinema, they opted for a CD, concert or film from New York New York.

Artistically, culturally, they campaigned for their city.

The only time Andy's future parents considered buying a work of art, they decided on a mixed-media piece signed by an artist everyone said was the perfect incarnation of a New York New York artist. They checked their finances and (with their finances checked) went to the gallery that represented him.

At the entrance of the gallery was a wood and resin reception desk whose seat and desktop had been merged into one single unit. It was the work of an artist whom the gallery had entrusted with designing the furniture. Its curved form allowed the public to immediately grasp its purpose. Behind this reception desk sat a young woman in front of a computer, on the back of which could be seen the logo of a cyanide-poisoned apple bearing the suicidal tooth marks of a homosexual mathematician. Following the persecutions the scientific community had made him suffer, the fag mathematician bit into the apple and died.

Unless, as his mother tells it, it was an accident owing to his propensity for storing chemical products all over his room. Unless we are supposed to see a morbid remake of *Snow White* in this gesture, which, according to legend, was his favourite film.

It was with complete indifference to this story involving chemistry, Snow White and homosexuality that the young gallery assistant was using this piece of technology. She paid hardly any attention to Andy's future parents, despite them standing there, hands behind their backs, hands in pockets, arms crossed, waiting to get someone's attention. With his fingers, Andy's future father started tapping in double and triple time on the desk's varnish. That infernal, rhythmic, plastic sound demanded only one thing: the attention of the girl behind the computer. Don't give a damn, she seemed to say. (This translation of young girl's thoughts is of interest only to the author.) She was completely absorbed in her computer screen.

At last, she raised her eyes. Yes? she said to Andy's future parents. This unexpected 'yes' began an exchange. In which they learned that this young woman, with her thoughts linked to her computer, was not the gallerist, and – get this – the gallerist wasn't a woman quite so young, but she was still quite a woman. A gallerist*a*. Briefed over the telephone about the intentions of Andy's future parents, the gallerista (we'll call her Suzanne) came down from her office up in the mezzanine and thus Suzanne, being the gallerista that she was, had them tour the exhibit while going on about the work of this young artist whose youth did not prevent him from having international fame but in fact quite the opposite.

Advancing through the exhibition, Andy's future parents stumbled upon the object of their desire. At a standstill in front of the piece, approaching it then stepping back in order to better comprehend it, they listened to Suzanne explain the intellectual approach the piece fit into, the visual-arts vocabulary it was based on, the artistic language it was an expression of, and above all the strength of the future work that would surely follow. After that, Andy's future parents received practical information regarding the conditions of the piece's production and the list of museums that had already solicited its loan. They felt the growing enthusiasm of those who are convinced of making the right choice. They laughed at the narration of anecdotes regarding the artist's psychology, his compulsions, his failings, his anxieties – right up until the announcement of the piece's price reduced them to silence. A fly buzzed around the gallery. Its vibrant trajectory monopolized our little trio. It's amazing how, in certain circumstances, the flight of a fly can be captivating.

The fly ate, vomited, ate what it had vomited, buzzed away, and Andy's future parents didn't say a word. Mrs. Andy puffed her cheeks, exhaled noisily, lowered her eyes and engaged in a meticulous examination of the state of her nails. Mr. Andy shuffled on the waxed cement, shifted his glance a bit to the right, a bit to the left, then into space. They cleared their throats in turn, for the sake of clearing them. As soon as they found sufficient resources to speak again, they announced to Suzanne, the gallerista, their intention to take some time to think about it.

Suzanne nodded. Wise decision, a purchase needs to be thought about. All the same, she advised them to not wait too long – they weren't the only ones interested. With a down payment, it was totally possible to reserve the piece for them.

It's funny, but as soon as Andy's future parents left the gallery, they realized that they'd completely forgotten to leave their contact information.

They had to face the facts: they didn't have the means for art from New York New York.

Despite this unfortunate episode, the future parents of John and Andy continued to identify with creations from New York New York. They sang, danced, read New Yorker New Yorkers. They saw New York New York everywhere. Anything that came from New York New York spoke loudly to them. They talked constantly to themselves about New York New York, and, better yet, they thought about it no less.

They worked a lot and had children.

John's parents and Andy's parents each had an only son, one named John, the other Andy. John and Andy were born in New York New York, received an exemplary schooling and completed a secondary education that was confirmed by the procurement of a diploma.

Andy began a career in visual communication. He drew shoes, boxes, vials, brushes, combs, pillowcases, washing machines, whips, toy-shaped weapons, weapon-shaped toys. You asked him for a toy, you got a toy. You asked him for a jewellery box, you got a jewellery box. Etc.

But after working for a few months, Andy had a change of perspective. Was it the passing of time that persuaded Andy to change? Or, rather, was it that Andy, taking the measure of time that speeds by no matter what, told himself he might as well take advantage of this momentum and change. One thing is sure, Andy did some soul-searching. Too many vials, too many shoes? Did he feel his work was being restricted to orders, formats and reproductions that limited his perspective?

If it's true that an artist is someone who produces things people don't need to have but that he (for some reason) thinks it would be a good idea to give them, then yes, what Andy made in his workplace was more art than visual communication.

Andy began to make series.

The first series bore the title *New Cumbersomes*. The principle of *New Cumbersomes* was to conceive of manufactured objects that all seemed to have been made in a factory but were all missing a piece vital to their proper function. They appeared to be in perfect working order, useful, functional, desirable, with no visual sign to betray their inadequacy. And yet ...

With this in mind, he drew a camera, from which he had a prototype made. The viewfinder worked correctly, it had a powerful zoom, multiple functionality, a perfect casing and was comfortable in hand. It wasn't digital nor was it equipped with a slot for film. Consequently, it was incapable of producing an image. How did you take a photo with it? You took the photo in your head, memorizing the moment it was shot, and that was it.

Andy came up with an automobile that had clean lines, a comfortable interior, contemporary design, thousands of gadgets that increased its value for dealers, except that the absence of power and a gas tank made it incapable of locomotion. It was an immobile car, a piece of junk good for racking up tickets along the highway before being impounded. How could an immobile car even claim to be called an automobile? It's about, Andy explained without losing composure, a car thinking like an automobile.

The second series was entitled *Surprise Objects*.

Look at this gun. Everything leads you to believe in its ability to hit the enemy; as you would expect, it's equipped with a butt, a barrel, a chamber, a bolt, a cartridge. It can be primed. It produces a detonation. It releases a bullet. It's blunt, it hurts, it kills. The shooter, god rest his soul, will learn upon using it that the shot is capable of turning against him. Until that final moment, you don't know in which direction the bullet will go. By introducing a dose of uncertainty, this weapon is the first to offer a rebalancing of forces. Before firing, the owner of the weapon cannot do without asking certain questions. Will the bullet hurt the enemy? Will it explode in his own face? Who will end up winning the duel? Who is right? The shooter? Who is wrong? The one who's shot?

In the same vein, there was the *Unwashing Machine*. That is to say, a machine whose functions seemed to comply with those of a classic washing machine, but whose cycles, thanks to a suction system of used water, worked to soil the laundry rather than unsoil it. There is no dirtier laundry than that which goes through this cycle.

Andy designed a stereo system whose aim was to be mistaken for a stereo system, the difference being ... what difference? Precisely. Andy preferred to keep the surprise. By unveiling the basis for the *Double-Murder Gun* and the *Unwashing Machine*, he's already said too much, and the same goes for we who report his intentions.

Andy launched himself into the development of a toilet that, through an inversion of the sewer system ... it was too much. Some clients complained. The artistic director acted responsibly. He spoke to the boss about it. Who told the principal shareholder. Who duly signed a letter drafted by his otherwise very charming personal secretary. Her name was Lisa, and she was the personification of a New Yorker New Yorker: elegant, cold, distant, and you realized to what extent once you got to know her and knew how to handle her. But let's move on.

Fired for a lack of sensitivity and misappropriation of supplies for personal use, Andy found himself without work or resources overnight. Without that subsidy helping him to subsist, without his mother to supply food and housing, it seemed like a good idea for him to go job-hunting.

Once out of school, John went wherever there was work. In an office located in the Business Quarter, which, for laughs, bore the name Wall Street, he put his knowledge of financial mathematics to use along with his ability to call the shots, his intuition for flow and his tremendous flair.

John offset the idleness that very quickly came from evaluating derivatives all day by making more and more overt advances toward Paul, a hot co-worker who was, my *word*, rather attractive. Paul was kind of seeing Lisa. You know Lisa, we just talked about her a moment ago: beautiful, tall, thin as a rail, executive secretary. All that to say that Paul had no taste for male homosexuality, even if it was purely verbal.

Bad luck: Paul's warnings had the gift of exciting John's desires. John abandoned symbols, forgot about metaphors and opted for more explicit words.

Let's take a closer look. John had sold his time to an employer, but all day during work he thought only about fucking. There's a serious explanation for that: John has a secret. John has a dick in his head. John is a man with two dicks. One lives in his briefs, the other in his head. And his boss didn't know that. The dick in his head worked for the dick in his briefs, and the least we can say is that when it came to working, this cranial dick *worked*. The dick in his head and the dick in his briefs understood each other perfectly, they agreed on the contents of their mission, they shared the same passion for a job well done, they did everything possible so that their projects worked out – they hadn't completed any long-term studies but their know-how was complementary, they hardly spoke to one another yet always understood each other, their collaboration was based on efficacy and synergy. They formed an ideal partnership. The world has rarely known such an efficient duo of dicks. For its mission, the dick in his head had to send an alert when potential prey appeared, liable for feeding its briefs-bound colleague, and it was up to John to go in for the kill. And so Paul at work was targeted. And the dick in John's head scrutinized his desirable body, devised situations and created possible schemes of ways for boys to love each other. Poor Paul. We won't tell you what happened to him in John's head.

It was John who, one day, decided to tell him everything.

What really amused John was the expression on Paul's face while John talked dirty to him. *Fist fucking, foot fucking* were the dirty words, the explicit words. Besides, explained John calmly, the words themselves imply the acts.

In order to flesh out his proposal, John produced some computer animations.

John has always maintained that to educate a heterosexual, every possible means must be used. Computers, among other things.

As a result, John was fired on the basis of extravagant sexual harassment against a financial analyst. Irrefutable. John found himself out of work, forced to live on a meagre compensation allocated by his former employer. What do I do now? he wondered in the evening while drowning himself in clear liquors. Recalling the short texts, the personal ads to meet men that he wrote during his free time and had published in specialized magazines, on dating sites, in forums, in public places, in parks, in halls, in the locker room at the gym, propositions that he graffitied on the walls of buildings, that he carved on public benches, recalling the texts he would slip into library books when he was returning them, texts whose composition evoked a style of free verse, texts brought to life by a density and tension that bore more than a passing resemblance to poetry, he decided to focus: he would reinvent himself through poetry, he would become a living poet.

3

Three friends look for and rent an apartment. They find themselves living together as friends who, wanting to become inseparable, wouldn't have it any other way. In order to talk about friends, at least two are required – in this case there are three, one more than the friendly minimum, which says something about how things stand between them.

Three is the perfect number, the golden digit, the welcome combination. So that we'll be convinced, let's repeat it three times.

Once.

Twice.

Thrice.

Three is the magic number in the sense that, more than any other, it allows for a possible roommate situation. Say three to a real estate agent and you'll see the magic happen.

It's sort of like summer now. There's an anachronistic warmth to the air. A totally out-of-season cloud of moist heat has descended upon New York New York. At the same time, there aren't any seasons in New York New York. The three friends have just moved into this apartment that fits this perfect figure, this number three that corresponds to them so well. Their apartment is located downtown.

The roommates are three out-of-work artists. But John, Bob and William haven't always been unemployed. In the past, they had salaried jobs from which they were fired, all three for the incompatibility of their morals with their professional environments. For making jokes that non-sodomites were not ready to hear, they were kicked to the curb. And on the curb, poor guys, unemployment awaited them.

After a time of collecting unemployment, they were due for back-to-work training. Or even to get new jobs altogether. Except they had it in their minds to make their unemployment last. Now, to make unemployment last – to not go to the employment office to get another job – in other words to play dead, to refuse work, to say fuck that to the working life – puts you outside the law. When did you ever hear of people being allowed to do fuck all in New York New York?

In order to rent the apartment, the three friends produced fake work contracts. As far as the rental agency was concerned, Bob was a self-employed tiler, John a freelance croupier and William claimed to be a part-time secret agent.

Fake names on the documents, fake documents, fake work contracts, no work, a little bit of money saved and a whole lot of free time.

The apartment of the three out-of-work friends has three bedrooms. One for John, one for William, one for Bob. Which says something about the quality of their relationship with their living space. Everything would have been absolutely perfect if the apartment hadn't been equipped with a fourth room, which also happened to be the biggest one of them all. What do you do with a fourth room when there are only three roommates? A problem arises. It calls for a solution. Bob?

Bob: Most importantly, we must baptize this room. First let's give it a name – guest room, workshop, foyer, storeroom – whatever we like. Its function will follow.

Three brains reflect on it.

Upon reflection, they agree that: 1) enough with the numbers already! 2) this big white room with skylights and columns stabilizing the structure will bear the name the Workshop, 3) for furniture, they'll use mismatched chairs, a hand-me-down sofa and upside-down crates for coffee tables. All's well.

Soon after the Workshop's creation, the three friends claim they love this idea of a common area, a space to collect as many things as possible, beginning with their free time. They spend their days in the Workshop doing this and that. No activity, thought or daydream goes unshared. They form a community of minds. The three friends think, write, draw, cut, ass-fuck, though not necessarily in that order.

The three of them (John, William and Bob) make up one of those groups of friends who are always heading in the same direction, walking side by side or strolling along single file. Inseparable, always together, whatever they do, and even if they aren't doing anything, no big deal, they're still together. The moment you see one, you see the other two. The threesome: there is no better name.

According to our calculations, each of them spends on average twenty hours a day in the Workshop. Multiplied by three, that makes sixty hours of daily presence in a single place, even though a day has only twenty-four of them. Go ahead and say that isn't just like working.

When it comes down to it, there's hardly any time other than the evening when the three roommates agree to leave the Workshop, where they have so many things to do, where they are so at ease. Because in New York New York, there's always something to do in the evening. And even when you think there isn't ... well, no, there's never nothing, there's always an art exhibition that needs opening.

An 'opening' designates the start of an art exhibition. And exhibition spaces are just like apartments. As if you couldn't inhabit a space without first inaugurating it with a party, without organizing a time for encounters between people who are pleased to see each other again or enjoy meeting one another between the installations and the buffet, glass in hand, mouth full of microwaved sausage, and something on their minds.

The three friends go to all the shows. They want to see as many of them as possible, to know what's been done and by whom. No downtown opening escapes their curiosity. They're in a basement gallery, in a warehouse, under an archway, in a hall, in a cellar, in a stairwell, in the lobby of a building. They turn up in an apartment that's thirty square metres, twenty-two square metres, sixteen square metres. They're at a group show organized in a hotel room. You'd believe them to be in a hotel room looking at and commenting on the pieces on display, but no, they've already dashed off to a screening of artists' videos in an underground parking garage. Standing in some dark room, in a neon-lit basement, glass in one hand, the other busy with the quickly vanishing finger foods, when the sudden proximity of a muscular body that would be nice to stroke requires the immediate liberation of a tactile organ.

Hey there. Haven't we met before? What do you think of the show? You wouldn't happen to be a friend of ... ? You have any plans later? You know about the Workshop parties, right?

Ah, the Workshop. Within a few weeks the Workshop has become known to all the out-of-work artists. And, in other words, to all of the opening-goers who make up downtown. Artists, gallerist(a)s, critics and writers, all non-professionals, come to the Workshop when the openings are over, when there's nothing left to drink, when the alcohol stash has been wiped out and they're still thirsty. No need for an invitation, accreditation, badge or who knows what – it's enough to push open the front door and say: Hi, I'm here, it's me, I brought a bottle of something but my pockets are also full of drugs made by a little hyper-specialized manufacturer in the office below my place, he's super-particular about the quality, he only makes a limited amount, now that I've tried his shit I only go to him, take this with a shot of vodka, wait twenty minutes, then tell me what you think.

The parties go on for a good part of the night. The last one to leave shuts the door behind him, a sign that it's over for today before it starts again, the next day, at the same time, with the same open-door policy and group high.

Initially a place for nighttime sociability, fuelled by booze, drugs, smoking, music and dancing, the Workshop very quickly turns into a place for sexual antics. There is music, which means dancing: there is movement, which leads to contact, which means touching, which means fondling, which means groping; the temperature rises, T-shirts stick to skin, arms raise, humidity soars, a boiling-hot spirit possesses all the participants. And it doesn't stop there: bodies undress, clothes fly, music wails, dancers respond by wailing, hands find their way onto others' bodies, now everyone is completely naked. The orgy begins. Code name: letter A.

The letter A. The first letter in the order of alphabetic appearance. A for ass-fucking.

Ass-fucking is one of the components of love between man and man, between man and woman, between man and animal. It can include love or even lead to love, or because it can be done without consequence, you can just ass-fuck for the sake of taking it up the ass, ass-fuck and then you're done.

Think of ass-fucking like you would anything else – certainly it's more of a pain in the ass, but other than that it's the same as any other thing.

Ass-fucking is optional, and, like the letter A, left to the user's discretion. It's practised with mutual consent, and because it's pleasant and good, it's subject to the approval of all the sodomite roommates: you can take it up or ban it, recommend it to your friends or prohibit its practice, saying, No sir, no ass-fucking here, I will have no ass-fucking under this roof.

By common consent, the three friends have decided to get some for themselves. They said yes to the use of the letter A in their pad. In this era, in this part of the city, among those who make art and are unemployed, ass-fucking with an A is all the rAge.

Ass-fucking, art, unemployment: the ideal trinity.

There are two types of sodomites: those who give and those who receive. The three friends belong to both categories. If sometimes the three friends fuck each other in the ass, this act occurs on the basis of a solid friendship and a mutual admiration that no botched ass-fucking can jeopardize. The proof: William loves John's poetry, John loves Bob's art, Bob loves William's prose, William considers Bob and John to be true artists, John and Bob think it isn't possible, in this part of the world, in this day and age, for there to be anyone more intelligent than William.

Jonas shows up and the group changes its name. Three plus one equals four – you can't argue with math. With Jonas added to the others, the threesome turns into a foursome.

On top of being the fourth friend, Jonas is also the man with the video camera. If you catch sight of a man behind a camera in the apartment of the three friends, you can be sure it's Jonas.

Jonas is a little bit like John, but without an h in the middle, and with *nas* at the end. How's that for lexicology?

Jonas and his brother share a stylish ground-floor apartment on a street parallel to the Workshop. A thin drywall partition separates the apartment into two tiny rooms, more or less equal in terms of living space. It's always dark in there, too hot or too cold, the air reeking of moisture. That said, Jonas couldn't care less. He's only ever home to sleep. Most of the time he's gone. Video camera in hand, strolling around, making friends who introduce him to their friends, and then together they make a film among friends until fatigue overcomes them. Then Jonas turns off the video camera, goes home to go to bed, and in his dark room he dreams of his film.

The material for the sociable Jonas's films is made up only of encounters between people – he doesn't film anything other than people meeting, dating, breaking up. Jonas's brother was a recurring figure in the first films but, since he hardly ever goes out except to go to work, he's no longer a part of the cast. As inseparable as the two brothers were for such a long time, now they just bump into each other sometimes: Hello there, my brother, how's it going? with a polite kiss on the cheek and nothing more, end of story.

Jonas and his brother come from a small village located in a traditionally little-known country. It's one of those landlocked countries difficult to locate on a map. It's one of those countries whose name is hard to spell, which can't be pronounced without also mispronouncing the name of its inhabitants. But even if a lot isn't known about it, it's one of those countries people can't help but have some idea about. It is, they say, a country whose inhabitants never venture beyond its borders. Not because they would have to leave in some clandestine way – it's because of the well-known poverty that seems to reign over the land that no one thinks about going on trips to places they can't afford.

It was while cutting across fields of rubble that the two brothers began a trip of their own, a trip to a foreign country. When their path, as risky as it was, crossed a train station, they boarded a train and took the first unoccupied seats they saw. Ignorant of the rules of public transportation, they hadn't thought to buy a ticket. We no understand language. We not know read well. We writing like dogs. Such is the story they told the ticket inspector. The inspector, not taking himself for the idiot they hoped him to be, stuck them with a fine and kicked them off at the next station. The two in-debt brothers reached the nearest town, where they had to resolve to take the first job that came along. They slaved away moving pallets for eight-hour shifts. Nevertheless, they earned money. They paid their debt to the railway and, with the rest of the cash, financed the next leg of their trip. They hit the trail. Oh, the towns they saw! They forgot them methodically, that is to say one after the other. Seen from a warehouse located in an industrial area, the towns no doubt resembled one another. Small towns: once you've forgotten one, you've forgotten them all. The way they tell it, the two brothers had to change languages multiple times, to become accustomed to new ways of lugging around pallets, and to get their ears accustomed to new ways of being called every name under the sun by the nasally voice of a bastard foreman. Still, wherever they were, they found a way to scrape by, making use of their willingness to work. They moved a lot, using a large variety of means of transportation. They travelled with no destination in mind. They left wherever they were at season's end with the feeling of having accomplished their mission, or rather what was done was done and no longer needed doing. A nice-sounding name was enough to make them stop in its corresponding town. At one point, they almost considered settling down somewhere. It's hard to say what was going through his head, but one day Jonas invested what little savings he had into the acquisition of a secondhand video camera. This tool gave a new direction to their wanderings. From then on, the desire to film would guide their trip. Along the way, they hit New York New York. So many places to explore, so many images to capture, so many friends for a night or longer. This city was made for Jonas to film. As for his wet blanket of a brother, once he settled down, he no longer wanted to go out. These adventures had exhausted him. Shortly after his arrival into the city, he found an honest girl, and as he himself was an honest boy, together they formed an honest, self-sufficient couple. They spent their free time just the two of them, staying at one's place, staying at the other's, nobody between them. There's no denying, they convinced themselves each evening upon returning from work, there's no place like home.

At the end of this journey, we are able to confirm that these two, Jonas and his brother, form what we'll call a family. A what? A family. Never heard of this word. Oh, well, a family is a unit in which ass-fucking is forbidden. In no instance did Jonas nor Jonas's brother ever give themselves over to it, not even with a third party. No big A for the Jonas brothers, but rather a J as in Jonas, and a C as in camera.

At the sound of this letter, Jonas turns on his camera and films the opening where the group has led him.

This evening, the art lovers have arranged to meet in a space that's about sixty square metres. Rumour has it that this apartment has been empty for years, that the landlord is a filthy-rich old man who owns so much of it – real estate, that is – that he's forgotten about this one. Young artists have set up there. They've made it into a place for living and a place for exhibiting. They'll stay as long as the authorities will tolerate them. A day will come when the landlord will wake up, react, get angry. A day will come when the young artists will be forced to leave and hit with a crazy fine, which will forever dissuade them from squatting on others' property. But before this cruel denouement happens, a groovy opening is taking place this evening.

Camera on his shoulder, Jonas moves through the dense crowd, which is excited and talkative. The space has plenty of people, plenty of noise and plenty of atmosphere. No sentence is audible from beginning to end. Bits of comments emerge related to the opening: This is a nice event, I'm glad we came, we should actually come back to see the work, because it's difficult to squeeze through to see this 148 x 79 x 68 cm wooden, fibreglass, polyurethane rubber and fabric sculpture, depicting the artist stretched out on a bed, awaiting death in various positions derived from some religion, like, for example, Catholicism.

The video camera moves forward, inviting itself into groups' discussions. Depending on the discussion and the people, some gladly offer their smiles to the camera, others turn away or get quiet. Suddenly, the camera catches a strange light. It's a full head of hair or a man-sized Christmas tree. It seems to be moving. It looks like a head. A head with decorated hair: silvery, coppery, shimmering hair, gilded hair that glistens, shines, sparkles, with a thousand variations at the light's whim. Party hair. Gay hair, joyous, resplendent, cheerful. It's even more beautiful at night.

Under this hair is Andy.

Andy who?

Andy, the new friend of the group.

Before becoming the group's friend, Andy had no friends. During the day, he saw no one except the woman with whom he shared a three-room apartment, who happened to be his mother. People say that during this time, Andy received regular visits from a guy named Dennis. Apparently, Dennis was one of those half-philosopher, half-art critic types who enjoys prowling around art openings and artists' studios. Andy had met him while he was still working in communications, and at that time, Dennis was frequenting comm agencies. Dennis is also the kind of guy you see all over the place – can't go anywhere without running into him. Being up-to-date on everything, Dennis enjoyed the story of Andy's sacking, and wanted to let him know that, so he expressed a desire to speak with Andy, who, having no friends, agreed to let Dennis hang out in his bedroom-workshop.

Upon seeing Andy's drawings, Dennis stated, Not bad, delicate lines, undeniable talent as a colourist, sense of composition, bravo ... it's cute ... there's certainly sensitivity and a technique, but on the other hand, addressing Andy directly, finishing his sentence with a snicker, but if it's art you want to do, then you're not there yet. Andy expressed his desire to become an artist, to which Dennis said, Okay, now, pay close attention. And Dennis, the talker that he is, gave a speech showing Andy that it would be judicious for him to work in a certain way, in the process adding two or three pieces of advice regarding his way of being Andy. You will be loved, you will be hated, he concluded by way of a prophecy, showing his naked body and trembling with desire for an unfazed Andy.

Following this studio visit, Andy seemed to work on his artistic expression, keeping Dennis posted on his progress with almost daily telephone contact. Up until the day Andy asked Dennis to visit, claiming he had a few things to show him. After pouring a thick and amber-coloured drink into a whisky glass, a glass he then handed to Dennis, Andy sat him down in front of two works on canvas, depicting two plastic bottles that at first glance looked identical.

And as the story goes, Dennis observed a long moment of silence which he then broke with a long critical commentary, of which Andy didn't miss a word, scattering in some *why?*s so that Dennis would say more, fully elaborate his ideas, explain his remarks to the fullest detail in order to achieve the clearest articulation possible, the most intelligible train of thought, using wording Andy would easily be able to reuse the day someone asked him to present his approach in a few short, memorable maxims.

By all accounts, meetings between the two boys became spaced out after that. They planned a series of appointments, which they cancelled. They communicated less and less until they ended up not speaking to each other at all. Andy and Dennis stopped thinking about each other. They lost touch for good.

Andy spent the following months in his bedroom where he drew, painted, decoupaged and coloured. Stretched out on a floor covered with newspapers, magazines, picture books and cut-up texts, with two different radios playing two different radio stations, he read and daydreamed.

After researching the lives of other artists from other times, from other places, Andy thought about his own situation. What could make him an original artist, an artist different from other artists? What if, on the contrary, Andy decided to become a non-original artist, i.e., an artist like some other artist? Andy told himself he could imagine becoming like some other artist. Which led him to the following problem: what is some other artist like? Andy wasn't unaware that a good number of artists existed before him, some of whom were named Andy. However, is homonymy enough to ensure similarity to his models?

During that evening's opening in a squatted apartment, Andy took a tour of the exhibition, then designated a corner for himself. He said, This here is my corner, and he went to hide out. He did what one does when one is shy and finds himself in a place where he doesn't know anyone and everyone else seems to know each other: stand off to the side, observe the surrounding opening-goers, listen, take notes. But given the present company at this opening, there is no corner in which to go be forgotten. There's still a video camera lurking.

Upon entering the shot, Andy was immediately offered an interview. Andy loves the idea of an interview. But he really prefers to ask the questions himself ...

Andy has developed a protocol that allows for an answer to be formulated before the question is even asked. Andy gives three possible responses in advance: yes, no, I don't know. The trick is to choose a response beforehand, and stick to it when you find out the question.

Andy: Yellow?

Jonas: Yes.

Andy: Black? White? Red?

Jonas: Yes.

Andy: Blue? Green? Yellow?

Jonas: No.

Andy: No?

Jonas: I don't know.

End of interview.

You know, Andy, I have these three friends, they have an apartment with a Workshop, what would you say to having a look around? Jonas proposes.

At one time there were four on the sofas in the Workshop, but now there are five. Five friends who stay warm by huddling together. About the five friends: three of them seem to be especially talkative, maybe because they're especially high. Andy, who is also high, doesn't say anything. Jonas films the encounter. As a result, the five men truly understand each other very well, and all are mighty happy with the evening. So why not become friends? What's stopping us from being together all the time?

Why not form another group that we'll call the fivesome?

This evening, like every evening, the Workshop fills up. People come and go. Naked when they come, dressed when they go. Andy remains pensive. Attentive to the night's proceedings, but pensive all the same. No one notices him, but he, from where he is, misses out on none of the night's proceedings. His job is that of the watcher. In his hands is an anachronistic camera. The type of instant camera they called a Polaroid back in Andy Warhol's day.

Suddenly a very muscular boy offers his services to Andy.

It's very kind of you to have thought about me, but ass-fucking isn't my cup of tea. I prefer not to do it. I prefer to watch.

I prefer to photograph.

I prefer to work.

I prefer to watch John.

Speaking of John, he uncaps his umpteenth bottle, downs it in one swig, and while opening another, performs some dance moves. Or what, for lack of a better term, we'll call dance moves. A remarkable work of disequilibrium and disarticulation performed completely off-rhythm. A way to defy the laws of physics. A dance that is impossible to reproduce without risking injury. John will end up falling. He's going to fall for sure. He's going to fall. He's falling. Hey! No. Phew. That was a close one. Bravo, Bob, nice reflexes. You all right? John starts up his moves again. Better to speak of 'moves' as opposed to dancing – he wind-mills his arms above his head, his legs bend and straighten, his pelvis turns, accelerating like crazy as if he were getting ready to take off. He's doing the helicopter. What's that, you ask? The viewer is invited to measure the distance between the comedy and pathos. All of a sudden, he's had enough. Stop. Enough. He's beat. Cut the crap. Eyes half-closed, John staggers off the dance floor, parting the crowd by giving little shoves with his shoulder, which he accompanies with, Pardon me, please, quickly, get out of the way, watch out I'm gonna puke.

But no, it was a joke. Just the magic words to clear a path through a dense crowd in order to get to an empty spot as quickly as possible. Like, for example, over here in this corner of the room where John squats to breathe. Now his back is to the wall, legs stretched out, eyes closed, neck loose, head drooping forward, back sliding down the wall. Laid out on the floor, John only has to spread his arms out in a cross and everything will be fine. John sleeps.

It's late. Andy is walking home. It's raining, or rather it has rained, the pavement bears a trace of recent dampness. Andy doesn't really care that it has just rained. Andy's head is somewhere else. His head is with John. Andy is thinking about this John who is capable of going to sleep in public. And then Andy thinks about Andy. Andy thinks someone is following him. Andy looks back. A woman is walking behind him. She has long, very brown hair, black eyes and olive skin. The reason she is there is to kill Andy. She's there as Andy's assassin. She's walking in the same direction as her prey, ten or so metres back. Andy's frightened. Andy speeds up his pace. He looks back. The assassin's long brown hair shines in the street lights. The woman acts like she's the one walking home, she pretends to be cool while on the inside the passion of her crime possesses her. A voice inside her repeats: you're here to kill Andy, you're here to kill Andy, kill Andy, kill him. She knows she's Andy's assassin, Andy knows it too, in fact everyone is in on it. But what is she waiting for to commit her crime? Andy hails a taxi, the taxi doesn't stop, and Andy concludes that the taxi is the brown-haired woman's accomplice. It's useless to try and escape an arranged death that even the taxi drivers seem to be in on. A few more minutes and Andy will be dead, assassinated. Andy thinks about John again. Andy clears the idea of taking a taxi from his mind – it's true, why take a taxi when you live just around the corner. Andy walks along 14th Avenue, turns at the intersection of 3rd Street. Andy arrives home to his mother. That's when he looks back.

Andy has an extremely precise concept of his death. He sees it as violent and spectacular. With New York New York being a very large city, Andy tells himself that there inevitably exists someone who would like to kill him. Either someone who has considered killing him for a long time and will one day do the deed, or – and this is the solution Andy holds on to – someone circumstance will put in a position to kill Andy, who will say, hey, why not assassinate this guy, and this someone, to his own great surprise, will take pleasure from the fulfillment of this act.

And the next morning, at breakfast with his mother, Andy considers that perhaps his demise is not all that imminent. For the time being, he's dying of hunger. What are we having?

From deep inside a pocket of a pair of men's pants, a telephone rings.

It's an outdated model that was never cutting edge, in any case. When it came on the market, its fun blackberry-coloured keyboard allowed it to be distinguished from competing models. For a time, the salespeople found it entertaining to promote a phone that was fresh and joyful in the eyes of their youngest clientele, up until the technological discussion was taken over by a generation of subscribers concerned about performance and features. In all honesty, because it's so inexpensive, this second-rate phone barely makes a profit. It was a good product for making calls, but its job is done. It's been ages since it was for sale anywhere in the city.

The telephone we are talking about is one of the last of its kind to still function. It spends most of its time in the patched pocket of a pair of low-cut, straight-leg men's pants made from a 98 percent cotton, 2 percent spandex mix, a flexible faded material. Along with a telephone, the pants pocket houses a lighter, some tobacco, rolling papers and filters, sometimes accompanied by a handkerchief, a used subway card and small amounts of change.

The telephone sees light for only a few minutes a day. And not necessarily every day. It befalls the phone to stay in the man's pocket for several days straight, sometimes spending a full week in darkness, silence and contemplation. For a telephone, it's not exactly overworked. It lives to the rhythm of a small cellular plan that allows only for short conversations. Most often, its job is to link two people who are trying to find out where one is, where the other is, and how they're going to meet up. Another one of its missions consists of ensuring communication between two people whose way of loving seems to be compatible, as far as they understand, and now wish to take action.

Today, the phone is responsible for a mission of the utmost importance. It's taking it to heart to ring its alarm for this man, this wreck of a human trying to prolong his night on a sagging couch, in the aftermath of a party, among scattered cans, a sticky floor and the odour of stale smoke. Its screen says 1:02 p.m. The sleeping man has to wake up. Which is why the telephone goes off with such conviction. It puts all the power it can behind it and, as if that weren't enough, it also begins to vibrate. The vibrations cross the cotton-spandex fabric, carrying through to the snoozing subscriber's thigh, provoking muscular tension on that spot, which quivers, and soon the vibrations reach his balls and then, almost simultaneously, his anus. Once the subscriber gets a hard-on, he wakes up.

It's high time to get moving because at 4:00 p.m. John is expected to be at the Centre for Public Poetry, where he's been invited to read his work.

A place of creation and dissemination for contemporary poetry, the Centre for Public Poetry organizes public readings, meetings and exposure to magazines and editors for both living and dead poets. The Centre offers thematic colloquiums, consciousness raising, writers' residencies, presentations abroad and translation workshops. To top it off, there's also a specialized library.

The Centre postulates that poetry isn't dead, and neither are the poets.

In poetry, as elsewhere, there is only one first time. Same thing for the second – no matter what they say, it's still unique. It's at the Centre for Public Poetry's Seventh Unpublished Poets' Night that John does his first reading.

It's happening here, come on, hurry up, get inside, it's about to start, find a seat, turn off your phones, it's starting now.

The room is plunged into darkness. White face, steady breathing, muscles relaxed, standing under a halo of light behind a microphone, illuminated, amplified, John has just walked onstage.

An hour ago, a knot formed in his stomach. It hasn't stopped growing, so now it's risen to his throat. But John knows that once his first word is delivered his throat will unknot and meaning will flow. He knows why he is there, he knows exactly what he has to do. He's ready to give it his all. He's ready to open his mouth and his heart, he's ready to open his mouth and his heart. Tonight he is John the Poet.

The four other members of the group take up the second-to-second-to-last row of the room. Andy is to the left of Jonas, to the right of Bob, and William is beside Bob. Guess to whom the hand resting on Bob's thigh belongs. A clue: it's moving up his thigh to draw a W around B's fly.

In the darkened room, Andy removes his glasses. He smells very strongly of cologne. John, in the light, standing, behind a microphone, inhales, looks at his text, opens his mouth and starts the evening off.

Reading.

(...)

Unpublished poet number two, Michael, facing the audience, reads standing up, behind a microphone stand, finishes reading, leaves the stage, applause.

Unpublished poet number three, Cecile, facing the audience, reads sitting, reads standing, behind a microphone stand, finishes reading, leaves the stage, applause.

Thank you all for coming!

End of the Unpublished Poets' Night.

The chairs, folding onto their velvet seat backs, produce the clacking of velvet.

The poetry lovers head toward the exit or in the direction of the guest poets.

Any comments?

It was very good, spot-on, had some rhythm, not boring at all. Right from the start we felt that you have something, a way of doing things that only you can do. The text is good, simple and good. You know, we get so many poets here who. And who've been doing it since. All right, well, I'll shut up. No, well done. For real, this was your first time reading in public? For a first reading, frankly ...

Superb. Fantastic. Marvellous reading. The room empties out, Andy, Jonas, Bob and William are still congratulating their friend. Soon, they're the last ones in the room. Before shutting off the lights, the organizer invites the five friends to move into the next room, the layout of which instantaneously summons a very strong sense of familiarity.

It's an exhibition room.

It has a bar.

For the exhibition, some poems are hung on the walls, shelves house some books, glass showcases display journals and posters. The whole thing is organized into an exhibit retracing the history of poetry in New York New York. We're going to take a look, Jonas, Bob and William let it be known before disappearing.

Over by the bar, John is downing one glass after another. He drinks indiscriminately – what's important is to drink. The thing is that this evening he's a poet, and for him, as it is for Andy who is standing by his side, that's strange to hear. John doesn't speak, he's feeling empty, empty and alone – perhaps that's why he's drinking, in order to fill himself up. His cup barely has enough time to be empty before it's miraculously full. There's no need to believe in divine intervention. No, instead it's the intervention of this guy in a dark suit, who, with a determined stride, heads towards John, plants himself between John and Andy – now there's an undeniable fact.

So then, you want to do the whole poet thing, the guy declares.

My goodness, um, poet, I, you know.

Listen, I have some news to give you. Allow me to introduce myself: I'm the Oracle of the evening. Ten years of experience serving living poets.

Which means ...

Rest assured, my services are entirely free. Oracle, it's more than a job, it's a passion for serving living poetry.

In that case, go ahead, we're listening.

The Oracle: Poet, in your adolescent bedroom you wrote a poem intended for some sort of pagan god. You did not imagine readers of poetry in any human form, only spirits were able to read you – poetry was, for you, the expression of a crisis that was resolved through the sacrifice of your oeuvre recorded in small spiral notebooks. During a ceremony personally directed by the author you tore up, burned, threw away the entirety of your poetic creations – farewell, literature. Poet, you are now an adult, your studies have led you to unemployment, you spent two whole years writing cover letters, and for as many letters you submitted, you received just as many negative responses. You've had unpaid internships, drawing on your experience you alternate six-month long contracts with periods of job seeking. Poet, seeing as you lack any prospect besides that of a life of sad and shitty jobs, you look for a solution to make life better – and you begin to write. Poet, while flipping through your city's cultural calendar, you learn that there are poetry readings, performance readings, performed readings, and in fact after more ample information it appears that a large number of today's poets read their texts in public. Poet, because readings are free, you go to them, alone for that matter, because not one of your friends is tempted by such an experience, and thus for the first time you see living poets. Poet, you attend as many readings as possible, you go see everything, you aren't picky, then again how could you be, you who know so few living poets. Poet, by reading your contemporaries at libraries and bookstores, by attending two or three readings every week, you are beginning to get a more precise idea of today's poetic practices. Poet, you discover an organized poetic environment, composed of active poets, publishing houses, journals, performance places and the promotion of living poetry, and you exclaim, So that's what I wanted to do. Poet, you get to know living poets, you are interested in the way they live poetry in an era that ignores it, you entertain the idea of devoting as much time as possible to making poetry, as little as possible to your boring and underpaid job. Poet, literature takes over your thoughts, you create texts while walking, you create texts on public transportation, you create texts while behind the wheel of your car, you create texts at work so as to mentally extract yourself from the computer-assisted production for which they pay you. Poet, when evening comes, you create texts in front of a muted television, in your bed you continue to write in your head, then it's bedtime, and if you don't want to feel tired at work tomorrow you should sleep but do you really care about not feeling tired at work tomorrow? Poet, you produce texts that you call 'my texts,' you work in a language you call 'my language,' you try to shape a literature you call 'literature,' you read out loud what is stuck in your head then you copy it on paper by hand before formatting and making corrections on a computer. Poet, you give the poets with whom you're acquainted texts to read and they tell you that what you write isn't bad, and in case you weren't aware it's called poetry so consequently you're one of them. Poet, you send your first manuscript to some publishers who publish poetry, meaning publishers who don't publish only novels. Poet, you await an answer with a mix of pride and anxiety quite characteristic of your psychology. You create different scenarios in your head, you fantasize about everyone celebrating your glory – yes let's be honest, your text is incredibly strong, there's practically nothing else to say, the book comes out and needless to say it's a success. Poet, your manuscript is returned with a letter signed by the editor that says you wrote a truly refined text that unfortunately does not live up to its potential, after the first forty pages you cease to invent, you dwell, what a pity, however dear sir you must keep at it, I sense a talented author in you, cordially, initialed, your manuscript will be returned to you under separate cover. Poet, this letter depresses you because it categorically refuses to publish your text as it is and you don't possess the critical tools that would allow you to make progress on it, you still don't know how to read like a writer must be able to. Poet, your disappointment is terrible, you say it's too hard, that you'll never get there, you try to summon the pagan god who during your adolescence followed your work attentively but he is henceforth unreachable. Poet, you lament your fate, you are very unhappy, your poetry friends console you by giving you the names of journals to which you could send your texts, they offer to put them in the proper hands, and there you go, after six months of waiting you receive your first positive responses. Poet, your poet name appears in journals' tables of contents, your bibliography is budding, yet you still complain that it doesn't contain the least little book, not even a booklet, you would like to see your name written on the cover of a work with a good publisher. Poet, you continue to write like a madman. Poet, for a long time now you've been writing unfinished manuscripts, but one day you feel like you have the perfect text, some people who've read it have said it's a good manuscript, a publishable manuscript, and after months consisting of highs and lows, half-assed promises, hopes slow to materialize, you find someone at a publishing house who takes on the publication of your first book. Poet and editor, you work the text thoroughly, discuss the cover mockup, choose a font, write up the back cover, print several sets of proofs on which you mark essential corrections, during this phase of the work you don't neglect any detail, and in the meantime you've signed a contract for three books. Poet, you sign for a package containing copies of this book which is your first, you invite your friends over and shell out for a party, the first book party – come empty-handed, everyone, tonight the poet is treating. Poet, your book hits the stores, and over the course of your visits to the bookstores in your city you lament that it can't be found anywhere, which is a slight exaggeration, even if it is true that very few bookstores carry it. Poet, after all the time it took you to write it and the difficulties you had to face before publishing it, you now have the impression that no one gives a shit, no one's reading it, no one's talking about it, no one's critiquing it, you can't fucking believe it, you're beating your head against the wall, but once again you're exaggerating. Poet, we regret to inform you that the only potential readers are other poets, being a few dozen people who, rather than purchase your book, ask you for comp copies. Poet, you calm down, you think it through coldly and you finally tell yourself that if no one knows living poets exist, how could their books sell? Poet, thanks to the support of this publisher that you like to call 'my publisher,' you publish other books that are the subject of critical reviews signed by top-level poets, poets who themselves have been the subject of numerous critical studies in their own country or abroad, and this time you can stop hiding, you are joyful, poetry is joy. Poet, there's a magazine that's going to feature you but it falls through at the last moment, there's a dissertation being written about you or more exactly a master's thesis, but overnight the student keen on poetry stops calling, and in the meantime, your name circulates around institutions, they invite you to contribute to literary events, you regularly have the opportunity to read your poems in public, you get a fee, your trip and lodgings are covered, you are paid and fed to be poet for a night. The readings allow you to meet poets, you make plenty of new friends and almost as many enemies, which you don't care about, you tell yourself that poetry is done between friends, you don't care about those assholes. Poet, interdisciplinary festivals give you the opportunity to come across dancers, actors, musicians, directors, plus a whole string of performers with whom you devise collaborative projects, some of which will even see the light of day. Poet, you no longer need introduction, poet, performer, you work on writing, sound, image, you make books and records, you play in groups, you appear in little video productions, you are physical, visual, acoustic, you produce poems in the form of lithographs, you make painted poems and drawn poems, you print poems on chocolate bars, tobacco pouches, curtains, sheets, lighters, pens, boxes of cookies, bottles of salad dressing, pillowcases, you publish poems in the form of small newspaper ads, you get hired as a demonstrator in a supermarket and you read your poems while giving out samples of mini sausages. You pirate advertisement inserts, you immerse yourself in written poetry, recorded poetry, exhibited poetry, you publish and you do live poetry, you double your collaborations with artists, you are in a large number of anthologies, they consecrate you with a second paperback printing, you become a hero in your field. Poet, another success in the bookstores and you'll be an accomplished writer. Poet, in agreement with your publisher, you decide to add the inscription 'novel' on the cover of your new book that's scheduled to be published at the start of the new literary season. Poet, if you think about it carefully, the line between poetry and novel is arbitrary, what it is you're working on is literature. Poet, the booksellers are not fooled by your 'novel' and shelve it in the 'art/poetry' section and as a result your 'novel' doesn't sell better than any of your previous books – don't worry, we won't reveal any numbers. Poet, it's too late to change your label, in literature you are a poet and nothing else. Poet, even for the hero that you are, you only have as many readers as an off-peak bus contains passengers, they say, He's known, for a poet – or rather, For a poet, he's known. Poet, these are the first nice days of the season, you're seated at a table on the patio of a café in the company of ten or so people, an improvised outing in a cultural place has put you in touch with people – about whom you know almost nothing – but you find them to be nice, and the feeling seems to be mutual, which is why you decided to get a few drinks together. Poet, you're caught in a round table, and when it's your turn to say what it is you do in life, you say, Hello, I'm John, I'm a poet. Poet, all around you people are laughing, I'm a poet, so you say, that's a really funny joke.

John: Bravo, I say!

Andy: Bravo!

The Oracle: Thank you! Glad you've enjoyed my performance. It's my big thing, every year I come play the Oracle for unpublished poets. The guys from the Centre don't support it, but they can't stop me. It's between performing the Oracle or the Biting Dog. I wanted to do a book to begin with, something along the lines of: *A Warning to Young Living Poets about the Misadventures of Today's Poets and Other Future Embarrassments Given Current Realities*. But seeing as no one wants to publish a text with such a long title, I perform it. Pretty good name, huh? Well, excuse me, I'll let you go now, I have to do the Oracle for some of the other Unpublished Poets.

John drinks and talks with Andy. John drinks more and faster than anyone else. He refrains from picking at the paper plates holding the kinds of foods that are edible in one bite. Eating is cheating. John devotes himself to the drink. According to his logic, one glass is immediately followed by another. At this pace, there's a tendency to not see time go by. John doesn't see time go by. In this kind of situation, people leave without anyone seeing them go. You realize they were right there with you the moment they're already gone. When they're no longer there and it's your turn to leave. The evening goes by as if time is passing more quickly for John than it is for the others. The exception being Andy.

John, he repeats, you're a poet now.

A window is open. Not all the way open – ajar. One pane is open halfway, an undeniable sign of a commitment to openness. On one side, the window looks out on a courtyard that's narrow and dark – dark because it's narrow – on the other side is a room that's bigger but just as poorly and shabbily lit.

Despite the darkness, it's still possible to read the 60 x 90 cm printed poem posted on the wall: TOO MUCH IS NOT ENOUGH. The room's furniture is limited to a mattress on the floor, a stack of books with a lamp on top, bottles that are empty or on their way there, a shelf holding clean laundry at the foot of which rests the dirty laundry from the day before.

The nightstand serves as a bookshelf. A bookshelf that has the characteristic of being upright and acting as a small nightstand topped with a lamp. The nightstand owes its existence to its proximity to a bed. Without the presence of this bed, there would be no talk of a nightstand, only of a small pile of books stacked on the floor. It's possible to sleep in this room. Thus, this room is a bedroom, for at least a few hours a day. Tonight, the bedroom is occupied. Someone is sleeping in the bed.

The sleeping man is named John.

As soon as he entered the room, he fell onto the bed, this single mattress tossed on the floor intended for resting. John curled up. He closed his eyes. He lost consciousness. He fell asleep.

John is sleeping in his day clothes. He's wearing a jacket, pants, shoes. He's dressed like he's getting ready to go out. He hasn't taken the trouble to undress, take off his clothes from the day and put on his sleepwear. He hasn't bothered to slip under the covers. That would have required too much effort. Too much time awake when the call of sleep was so pressing.

It's urgent to sleep like before it was urgent to drink. John drank a lot. In this immense metropolis, you have to run on something, whether it's alcohol or drugs. That's how it is in New York New York, a new drug every day, you have to have something that'll fuck you up and take your mind off everything. Like the time John saw himself going down the wild rapids of a river in five minutes flat. He wasn't really going down them. He was hallucinating. Five minutes of ecstatic rafting. It's not just something to talk about.

Andy is on amphetamines and as a result he's become a raging insomniac. His ashy-grey complexion and the bags under his eyes are proof that Andy's keeping up with this druggy bandwagon and, my god, is he keeping up.

Tonight the roles are broken down like this: John is sleeping, Andy is awake.

This is the first night that John and Andy are together, young lovers occupying the same bed. For once, Andy would have gladly done more, but now isn't the time – what a bummer. If there is a time for touching, a time to sleep together rather than go to sleep, that time has passed. You don't fuck a man who's sleeping. You follow in Andy's foot-steps and go limp. Unless. Let's murmur with him:

John?

John?

Jooooohn?

No response.

John is deaf to the sound of his name.

Because not only is he sleeping, the bastard is also snoring.

It's pointless to keep trying, realizes Andy while getting up from the double bed. Andy crosses the bedroom. He opens the window with an upward thrust from bottom to top, giving the handle a delicate push for an added personal touch. The bedroom window is open.

It's a window that opens onto a square courtyard, a dark hole that is home to a mess of bottles and cans, discarded objects thrown from windows, cigarette butts, cardboard boxes and wrappers. The popping of a detonation echoes. The whistling of a tracer bullet. Second detonation. Exchange of live ammunition. Gunfire. Yells. Shouts. Abruptly interrupted by the sweet music of a commercial break. The viewer mutes the sound. The return of automobile noises wafting up from nearby streets. They coalesce into one continuous vibration. Andy lights his cigarette, smokes it down to the filter and tosses the butt into the courtyard.

No two ways about it, Andy isn't sleepy.

Andy lights another cigarette. Smokes it down to the butt. A butt whose destiny is to be thrown into the courtyard. Andy closes the window. Andy walks around in socks on the wooden floor, to the extent that he ends up joining John in bed.

Okay.

And now, let's move on to the next sentence, which is: John plus Andy equals love.

John loves Andy because he's Andy. Andy loves John because he's John. John finds Andy very ugly. Andy finds John very handsome.

There's a problem: Andy hates to be touched. During orgies, Andy has always preferred to watch rather than participate. That bothers some people. John, on the other hand, likes to do. He does it well. He gives a lot of himself. He acts like one should in such circumstances: forward, energetic, generous, insatiable.

Yet all it takes is for John to decide to take his cock out for some fresh air and for Andy to grab it, take it in his mouth and start sucking. Then John closes his eyes and waits for what's coming. In these instances, John's face: a) tenses up, b) relaxes. An incontestable sign that: c) he's coming, d) he came. When all is said and done, Andy swallows and sucks again, John puts it away, the two friends move into the living room, take out a few bottles, arrange some bowls of chips and peanuts on the coffee table and talk about something else.

In day-to-day life, John and Andy don't hide that they love each other. Why should they? What about this love story is there to hide? Does anyone have an objection to it? If they wanted to kiss in public, they would kiss in public. Except Andy doesn't want to. If they wanted to hold hands in public, they would hold hands and walk side by side. Except Andy doesn't want to. They could perform all the public displays of affection, but Andy doesn't feel the need. Neither does John, for that matter.

In the meantime, some juicy gossip is going around at the openings. It's about John and Andy. Andy whom they no longer call 'Andy,' but 'Thing.' A nickname soon replaced by 'Wig.' Well, anyway, there's some crap going around. Supposedly, both of them. Like that, both of them? Where is the beginning of this sentence going? And what are their friends from the group saying?

Ah, the friends – well, well, let's talk about them. Let's talk about Bob's snickering, William's mocking. They feed on gossip, the traitors. You call them friends? It's true that, in the past, William tried to bang Andy. But William, despite his brilliance, his intellectual qualities and everything, is difficult to like. No thank you, Andy said. And William took this rejection poorly, despite it being done so politely. The day will come when he will make Andy pay. As for Bob, who's interested in John, he feels like he's losing him to Andy. No, Bob doesn't truly understand what John sees in Andy. He'll also find a way to get revenge.

Someone who right away seems to be very happy about this budding love between the men is Jonas – he's practically euphoric about it – to the point it looks like he's going to come out and ask John and Andy to form a love triangle. But there, you see, is where you're mistaken. An ardently friendly man, Jonas is simply happy that his two friends love each other. And he never fails to let them know. He's happy for them, because he considers John and Andy to be his friends, and there's nothing else to it.

Seeing as how people are turning their backs on them at the openings, you might think things are going to turn out badly. You might think that John and Andy are going to suffer because of the gossip that's being spread about them. That they're going to be hurt. Be affected. Bend under the attacks. And then what? Change addresses? Leave the group? Stay holed up at home? Split up? You certainly don't know them very well. Someone's criticizing them? They have a good laugh. At first they laugh. Then they think about it. Organize themselves and retaliate.

Andy has an idea. John, he says, you're appealing to women, you just need to seduce the ones who come to the openings with the misogynistic guys – it's a way to make them understand that you're ready to fornicate in retaliation, and you'll see that they'll stop making fun of us.

At the openings, John begins to make women laugh – all he has to do is talk to them. It's pretty simple: when they're with John, they have a great time. Good old John. And the non-fag men become buddies with him again.

They would rather John be a fag with Andy than the lover of an adulterous woman. How's that for Christian morality?

In short, Andy and John tell you to fuck off.

Life as a group continues.

—

This morning, Andy looks at himself in the bathroom mirror, and what does he see? He sees a guy with white skin, a thin body with very little muscle, always exempted from gym class in school, seemingly embarrassed by his body. Sickly-looking at the best of times, otherwise cadaveric. Today, while looking in the mirror, Andy catches a glimpse of a guy who says to himself: Unemployed artist, that'll soon be behind me. He sees a guy looking at himself in the mirror and says: It'll all pay off in the end.

On a side note, what is it that will end up paying off? Pay how, pay for what – so many unknowns. But in any case, in Andy's mind, given his morning mood, things are clear: this adventure will end up paying off.

Like every morning, Andy gets up early. Not unusual for a morning person. He has breakfast, hops into the shower, lathers up, scrubs, brushes, moisturizes. Two minutes later he is ready to face the workday, except there's one problem: he's hard. Because he is subject to a persistent stiffy, because he has to get rid of the thoughts making him hard, because they keep coming back and having the effect of further hardening the culprit, how far will he decide to go? He decides to go all the way.

All set for a sporty-erotic sequence, he takes the problem equipment in hand and instantaneously produces a two-voice narrative. Him: My, how hot it is under this uniform! Let's get comfortable. Me: Oh look, a naked Cuban soldier. Him: Hi there. Me: Hi. Him: Can I do something for you? Me: Uh, well you know, I really like to lick shoes. Him:

Great, that's my fantasy too. Me: Well, now that we've been introduced, let's not waste any time and get straight to the point. Him: Go ahead, lick. Me: One more thing, I like to be talked dirty to while I'm licking. Him: Okay, lick, you dirty son of a bitch. Me: I'm licking like a dirty son of a bitch. The Cuban soldier is totally naked, he's kept his shoes on, like in one of John's poems. Him: Oh, my dirty little son of a bitch, go ahead, lick it more, more, more, more, faster, come on. Me: One more moan for a finale, drops of sweat beading on my forehead, we're almost there, more, more, careful, stop.

Nice work, well done.

Andy can finally call John (voicemail). He leaves a message (are you sleeping?) then he goes back to work in his bedroom.

On the other end of the line, the telephone rings, rings, rings. The blackberry-coloured telephone produces an incalculable number of rings. To count them all wouldn't serve any purpose. That's why we're saying it was an incalculable number. To make a long story short. The telephone rang a first time, sending the call to voicemail. After which the telephone hasn't stopped reminding, soliciting its owner to listen to its recorded message, something to do with Andy's first call, don't you remember, the one from which all of this began. And, in the following minutes, the telephone reminded him, harassing the message's addressee. Because such is the logic of a telephone: make the user listen to the recorded message at all costs.

Andy's telephone can multiply calls to John, even while John is sleeping. And while he's sleeping, his principle is to never talk on the phone. When the time comes and he's awake, John will respond, but don't count on him to take the call before.

Solution: wake John up with a large number of rings.

At regular intervals, Andy calls again and leaves a number of repetitive messages (are you sleeping? are you sleeping? are you sleeping? what are you up to?), increasing the recurrence of rings, causing confusion between direct calls and voicemail reminders. Andy's Xth attempt to get hold of John is successful.

John: Yes?

Andy: John, I have an invitation!

John: A what? For where? What are you talking about?

Andy: John, you know what I'm talking about, I won't say anything else.

The invitation is for the opening at *M*useum. Anyone in a position to answer how Andy got hold of it – through what trade, chance or well-seized opportunity – must be very clever. One fine morning, the invitation found its way into his mailbox. And, a few minutes later, into his hands. That's the whole story. But that's not the main thing. The main thing is that the invitation is valid. And not only is it valid, but the invitation is for two. Andy shares the worrying message printed on the back with John:

CHIC OR SPORTY CHIC DRESS SUGGESTED

That day, because they didn't grasp what 'sporty-chic' meant, John and Andy, in everyday dress – leather, jeans, sneakers with two stripes – arrive at the bottom of a luxury building that houses *M*useum on the thirty-fourth floor. Equipped with their invitation, they present themselves to the doormen, Bill and Bull.

Gentlemen!, Bill decides after performing an ocular inspection of these two that he doesn't suspect of being unemployed. In a perfectly synchronous movement, Bull opens the door of the building for our two unemployed artists: Have a good evening, gentlemen.

The door of the building opens into a hallway. The hall leads to an elevator. In the elevator is a male-female couple. The thumb that was keeping the doors open releases its pressure from the doors-open button. The elevator starts to move.

Lowering their eyes as is required during elevator trips, John's and Andy's gazes fall upon the man's sneakers. While John's and Andy's are fitted with two white stripes on a black background, his have three, and on top of that they're silver.

Originally intended for the practice of a sport played with a racket, a net and a ball, Adas (two stripes) or Adidas (three stripes) were quickly hijacked for artistic and mundane purposes. They are, it would seem, perfectly suited for exhibition visits and any standing around that ensues, because in New York New York, a large number of opening-goers swear only by them. So the opening adopts a little sporty side. After indoor sports, gallery sports. Before the elevator episode, John and Andy were unaware that a pair of sneakers could have more than two stripes. Downtown, the Adas are considered the best as far as artists' shoes go. Uptown, an extra topstitched stripe gives the sneakers the right to sport a three-syllable name. One stripe per syllable, like a glamorous slope. Thus the secret of 'sporty chic' was solved: 'sporty chic' indicates a chic outfit worn with a pair of sneakers with three stripes called Adidas (it's written on the tongue).

The elevator comes to a halt. Thirty-fourth floor, chirps a bisexual voice. The door splits into two parts that mechanically disappear on either side. The four riders wish each other a good evening and, setting off in two groups, they enter *M*useum.

We find John and Andy each in possession of a glass full of a frothy liquid. Thus equipped, they decide to do the tour of *M*useum. Let's follow them. Something detains them in the hall. Guys carrying trays circle around them. The two friends play the game: they set their glasses down and pick up new ones, they make some friends, time to toast and take pictures before parting ways forever. John and Andy go to visit the exhibition.

The *M*useum introduces a great exposition of oil paintings on canvas. On the canvases, romantic heroes and other young people belonging to their era lounge about. The artist calls herself Elisabeth. The exhibition is entitled Eternal Life.

Max, Craig, Pierre, Walt, Marc, Rirkrit, Piotr, Julian, Walt, Frida, Liz and Diana, Keith, John, Jonathan, Matthew, Eminem, Patti, Nick, Nick in the East, Nick and Patti, Harry and Tittie, John and Sid, Silver Bosie, Kurt, Blue Kurt, Sleeping Kurt, Jarvis, Jarvis on a Bed, Jarvis and Liam Smoking, the plaques indicate. And there's still: *Madame Bovary, Antoine Doinel, Eugéne Delacroix, Napoleon, Prince Harry, John the Poet, Ludwig II of Bavière, Ludwig with Joseph, Ludwig Caressing the Bust of Marie Antoinette*. Etc.

With the help of champagne, the evening finally becomes pleasant. You wouldn't have thought it at first, but John and Andy seem to be at ease. Andy even manages to look receptive to the jokes that John has long told in vain, usually receiving only criticism from Andy. Which goes to show he's actually bored to death. He doesn't feel well, or at ease. He doesn't know what he's doing there. He doesn't know what anyone expects from him, and he almost even wants to run away. If he'd known, he would've stayed home. He would have slept for once. He would have gotten somewhere with his work. He would've watched TV. He would've spent the evening with his mother. I have no idea, but anything besides being bored in this *M*useum where everyone seems to know each other but he isn't known by anyone.

Wrong path, he says to himself, I'm right on track to stay unemployed.

And as the night evolves, we see our two friends in a playful, even comical, spirit – our two drunk friends who, completely buzzed on champagne-amphetamines, amuse themselves by finding doppelgängers in the crowd. They play the doppelgänger game with even fewer scruples since they don't know anyone. Since they don't have any connections. Since they don't have a reputation to keep up. Since they don't give a shit.

It's crazy how analogies are born under the influence of drugs and alcohol. John points out Max's doppelgänger. Andy, Billy's doppelgänger. John recognizes Lou. Andy finds a resemblance between a guy in a yellow suit and Candy. John refers to a tall guy whose skeletal body swims in a suit two sizes too big, and declares, I didn't know William was here.

Oh John, you exaggerate, replies Andy before bursting into laughter.

John is such an ass.

He's an ass, but there you have it. They work at finding resemblances, they're connecting existing faces with their lookalikes, they say, Look, there's Eleanor, and it really is Eleanor.

For those who weren't aware, they're actually at her place, everyone is at Eleanor's. In this building, Eleanor owns *M*useum on the thirty-fourth floor, the gallery on the thirty-third, the agency on the thirty-second, the offices on the thirty-first, the studios on the thirtieth. And on it goes until the second lower level (trash, cellars, crematorium, parking garage).

Eleanor. Because they've only heard Eleanor spoken of but never seen her, John and Andy have long believed that Eleanor was just a name. A legend who was given a name precisely to say she was a legend (in addition to being a name). Eleanor, woman in black, with a modern elegance, asymmetric dress, tar perfume, petrol-blue eyeshadow, anthracite lipstick, vampire skin. It's difficult to assign her an age, especially when you don't really care. John takes care of introductions.

John: John, Andy.

Eleanor: All right, and what do they do in life, this John and Andy who outright reject the dress code, pillage the bar and make fun of people?

John: I am John the Poet.

Eleanor: John the pOet? Nonsense, that sounds stupid, no one would believe it for a second – you'll never make a name for yourself, you're already screwed, think about a career change. And otherwise, what does he do with his life?

John: I'm a poet, that's all. I'm a poet looking for work.

Eleanor: Work for a pOet? He's looking for work for a pOet? For fuck's sake, you hear that, that's the best! Not only do I learn that pOets still exist nowadays, but this one, he comes and says it like that, I'm a pOet, give me work, how dare he, ass hole ass hole ass ass ass ass ass ass ass ass ass ass ass ass ass ass ass ass ass ass ass ass ass ass ass ass ass ass ass ass ass ass ass ass ass ass ass ass ass ass ass ass ass ass ass ass ass ass ass ass ass ass ass ass ass ass ass ass ass ass ass ass ass ass ass ass

A small group has formed around the trio. Smiles on their lips, glasses in hand, they follow the discussion with great interest.

John: I'm not picky, I'm adaptable, flexible, I can be a poet on demand, available now, ready to go – I would be happy to put my competences in the service of an art gallery. The small audience has a good laugh. John laughs as well. It's Eleanor's turn to speak.

Eleanor: Courageous, in any case, to make pOetry nowadays, I admire it for fuck's sake fuck's sake fuck's sake fuck's sake fuck's sake fuck's sake fuck's sake fuck's sake fuck's sake fuck's sake fuck's sake fuck's sake fuck's sake

John: In a nutshell, she loves poetry.

Andy: I'm not so sure.

Eleanor: Fuck Fuck Fuck Fuck Fuck Fuck Fuck Fuck Fuck Fuck Fuck Fuck Fuck Fuck Fuck Fuck Fuck Fuck Fuck Fuck Fuck Fuck Fuck Fuck Fuck Fuck Fuck Fuck Fuck Fuck Fuck Fuck Fuck Fuck Fuck Fuck Fuck Fuck Fuck Fuck Fuck Fuck Fuck Fuck Fuck

A minute passes. Filled with a great number of fucks. A waiter taps her on the back, takes a pill bottle from his pocket, dumps two pills in the palm of his hand, slips them down Eleanor's throat, with a tall glass of water, please.

Eleanor: Aaaaaaaaaaaaahh!

The waiter: Tourette Syndrome – don't worry, you shouldn't take the insults to heart, it's just the verbal manifestation of the sickness, the words come out all by themselves, people take offence when in fact it means nothing.

John: No problem. I didn't hear anything. Right, Andy?

Andy: Nothing at all, John. I wasn't even listening.

Andy has spoken. Eleanor fixes upon Andy.

Andy's turn to talk about his artist's life.

The scope of *Cumbersomes* and *Surprise Objects*, life with Mother, working day and night, the violent death that stalks him, the wearing of black sunglasses and glittery hair – it seemed to be amusing dear Eleanor. She appears intrigued. And while Andy is as usual completely elliptical, quasi-absent, it's actually John who is speaking on his behalf, and ultimately she'd like to take a look at some of his work, just to see what it's all about.

If it's possible to see it, for fuck's sake.

For fuck's sake, of course it's possible.

And now a business card, a meeting scheduled for next week, and Eleanor slips away repeating Andy, Andy ... Andy who?

Since we last saw Andy, several months have passed, immediately transformed into time spent working. Soon he had spent ten, twelve months working. It took the time it took – ten, twelve months exactly – but on the whole the work was done, the hours required were carried out, enough to meet the criteria for the required legal duration of work.

Andy has been a professional artist for twelve months now. This professionalization goes back to the day Eleanor let him into her gallery. Today Andy is an artist who is well-known, popular, collected. As a result, there is no lack of work. The days could last for seventy-two hours and he'd manage to transform them into working time. Andy produces prolifically.

Andy created the Studio, a production facility for which he hired two people, the kind who are former art students and/or unemployed artists. Recognizable by their long, or short, or dishevelled, or coloured hair, very messy and very maintained at the same time – proof that an art student and an unemployed artist share the same hairstyle, no matter their aesthetic options.

Out of convenience, they were christened Gerard and Gerard. Why Gerard? In Eleanor's opinion, it needed to be something easy to remember, something pleasant. If you see what I mean. No? Because it's cool at the same time. Sexy, cool, with a little artistic note. Still no? Listen, it's like this, they call both of them Gerard, so if you're not happy with then you can go ffffffffffffffffffffffffffff yourself.

Pill, glass of water. Where were we?

Since Andy first walked into the gallery, Eleanor has spread the idea that Andy is the artist New York New York has been waiting for. Her public relations done, Eleanor organized workshop visits, showing up regularly at the Studio in the company of collectors, critics, journalists, curators, museum directors, industry professionals, company heads. Plus a whole bunch of guys who made some dough where it is possible to do so – for example, not in the arts – guys she introduced to Andy and who left the Studio saying to themselves, What a funny guy that Andy is, to be so bizarre he must be a true artist. Would it be worth it to buy a piece from him?

This period of Andy's career is called the Golden Period. Andy sells everything he thinks. Andy sells everything he touches. Andy sells everything he signs. Andy sells pieces before they're produced, on the sole fact that they will be signed by Andy. Andy offers readymade and custom-made art. With Andy, you can have your heart's desires. Two or three-dimensional pieces, from monumental to infinitesimally small, choose your motif – choose your size, choose Andy. Andy promises to deliver within the record time of one week max. Give yourself the pleasure of having an Andy in your home. Transport and installation are also available.

Stop everything. It's all crap. I can't work like this.

His first private exhibition will take place in three months. It'll take place in the main gallery of *M*useum. And what will it be? What will be seen there? Andy hasn't the least idea. Every time Andy comes up with a new idea for an exhibition, Eleanor responds, That's good, and right away finds a collector to buy it.

Conclusion: you'll have to find something else for the exhibition, dear Andy.

Exhibit the *Cumbersomes*? *Surprise Objects*? No kidding that Eleanor really loves these works, that's why she'd rather keep them. Wait for Andy's name to raise their popularity, bring them out again and aha!

Aha! Andy is workless.

When all of a sudden, someone rings the doorbell.

Mother: Andy!

Andy: Mother?

Mother: John's heeere!

Quick, Andy's late, he has to finish doing his makeup, brush his teeth, get his things together, choose his glasses and jacket, dress his head with a platinum wig – or maybe a sparkly silver wig – hurry up choose something, let's say the sparkly wig, or not, or yes, both at the same time, let's see.

During this time, seated next to each other on the flowery couch in the living room, John and his mother-in-law attentively follow a television program. Jack is one question away from winning the super jackpot.

Jack, you've chosen answer B, is that your final answer?

Ah, here's Andy.

John and Andy hug Mother and leave. Their departure is accompanied by a gesture that means goodbye. Goodbye, Andy and John.

The evening begins with screenings of experimental films in the back room of a car wash. The screenings take place in a room that, officially, doesn't exist. In the old days the car wash was a cinema, but that is all over. It's the time of car washes, not cinemas. On the other hand, there's always some way to manage: having been a cinema, it can always be used as one again. Two and a half hours go by. The spectators are invited to leave through a hidden door. In order to not alert the neighbours, it was recommended that they not make any noise while leaving. Which they translated as walking on tiptoe, without saying a word, reserving their commentary for later. After a hundred or so metres of silent walking, tongues start to wag.

John: You were saying?

Andy: That was so boring! Why was it so boring?

John: I don't know. I slept through the entire thing.

Andy: John, tell me, why doesn't anyone make good films?

John: I don't know, Andy, what do you call a good film?

Andy: I don't know. I call a good film a film that's not boring.

And the two friends reach the Workshop for their usual party. A rumour has preceded Andy's arrival.

Andy?

Andy's here tonight?

But where is he?

Where did you see him?

You're sure it was him?

You know what he looks like?

How did you recognize him?

There, in the wig, that can only be him.

Come on, let's go meet him!

Barely in the door of the Workshop, Andy is surrounded by four guys. They're wearing plaid shirts, glasses with chipped frames. Unbelievably, they're all wearing Das, these sneakers with one stripe that just became popular among the young and very young artists. They're scruffy, hair styled to look unstyled, but really who are they? They claim to be artists. Very young artists who have seen fit to gather in an artists' collective.

Their artists' collective, we learn over the course of the conversation, is invited to participate in an exhibition whose goal it is to introduce a new generation, to take the pulse of the emerging sensitivity, to mark the points of intersection and divergence, and to participate in its influence on the international scene. In this strong engagement with young creation, it's a question of making its incessant mobility visible, its constant displacements from one media to another, from one discipline to another, in no certain order.

Congratulations! Andy declares.

Change of DJ behind the turntables. The sound is louder, more intense, more brutal. The very young artists formulate their idea of art to a hardcore musical background, and whisper it directly into the hearing canal of their silver-wigged listener. The same one with whom they establish a physical connection by laying one hand on his shoulder. Because of the competing bass, Andy doesn't hear much, just a few syllables that despite his efforts, he still doesn't manage to link. To be honest, he can't understand anything. The DJ raises an arm, leading the dancers to dance with raised arms. Andy looks for a friendly gaze. Andy is looking for a way to extricate himself from this conversation, which, really ...

And what about John?

Where is he? What's he up to?

The last time Andy saw him, John was eating and joking around, talking with some new friends he'd just met. They asked him questions. They asked him what he did in life. With a big laugh, he said that he sleeps.

The very young artists still have a few things to say. They yell out, Andy, what are your options? Do you have any projects? Any news? Any contacts to give us? Would you like to become our friend?

Andy: Well ...

(...)

Sorry, Andy must absolutely go see someone.

He's pleased to have met you.

Keep us up to date.

Best regards.

See you later.

Kisses all around.

Andy stumbles onto the dance floor, hints at a few rhythmic steps, takes a look around. No young artist in sight. However, in his position, you can't be too careful. Since he turned pro, he's in every conversation. Many artists want to talk to him so they can say that they know him or, more annoyingly, that they have plans to exhibit together. Lowering his eyes, Andy discovers that his new Adidases have been smudged. Fucking artists' collectives.

William and Bob follow him with their gaze. Jonas films. William: I know what we're going to do. Let's make a scene. Let's take advantage of the fact that a lot of people are in the apartment to simulate an unfortunate incident. Trust me, if done right, we can make it believable.

Bob: All right!

Seriously, where has John gone off to? Andy visits John's bedroom-turned-coatroom. John's not there, or else he's been reincarnated as a coat. Andy visits the other rooms, Bob's bedroom, William's bedroom, discovering you'll-never-guess-who in the middle of an affair with sorry-I-can't-really-say. But still no John. Andy's making himself anxious. Note the almost phosphorescent whiteness of his skin when, back in the Workshop, while passing under a spotlight, the light hits him smack in the face.

Good God, someone exclaims, it's a ghost!

Andy visits the bathroom, no luck, waits his turn for the crapper, because you never know and after all it's a place John likes to practise. Except not, no John in the crapper, it's Eddie who slips out. Andy takes over the space. Standing in front of the bowl, Andy takes his dick out and tries to piss. He doesn't need to go. What does he do now that he's already there? Instinctively, Andy jerks off. Obviously, this masturbation is doomed to fail because of its questionable motivation, so Andy changes his mind. Fly zipped, he goes back to the room where everyone is dancing their asses off.

At the edge of the dance floor, William and Bob wave to him. Andy responds by nodding his head.

Bob: And what if it's not a wig?

William: Then his natural hair colour would be sparkly silver.

Andy can't accept that this John who loves him and who he loves is capable of leaving the party without telling him. Without at least one word signifying his weariness, his boredom or a sudden wave of fatigue.

John, why'd you do that? If you love me, why did you leave me all alone?

Eddie: Do you dance?

Andy: I used to dance, I don't dance anymore, remember it was while dancing I had that terrible accident ...

Eddie: I can't hear anything! What accident? Come on, no excuses!

Andy: Yeah, well fine. Let's dance.

Eddie makes her bangs move as she dances. She does a dance only she can do: her bangs move first, her body follows the movement. Andy can't pull that off. He's just happy to do the Andy. Like a flexible post, stiff neck, twisting his ass.

William hands his glass over to Bob. They go ahead and have a laugh about the dirty little trick they've planned.

William approaches Andy, who has his back turned to him.

Andy's wig has never been touched by anyone. John, for example, is forbidden to do so. He's always considered Andy's hair to be on par with religious relics, taboos and pieces in a museum. It falls into the category of things on which he will never lay a hand.

William burlesquely loses his balance, stumbles onto the dance floor, bumps into one, two, three people, finding his balance one, two, three metres further, his hand resting on Andy's head.

The wig shifts back a notch, sliding toward the back of Andy's head. Enough to clearly distinguish the forehead and balding temple of its owner. Eddie stops dancing, puts her hand over her mouth. She hadn't seen the little bastard, so to her it's even worse. For a moment she seems to be holding in a laugh, but a moment later, explodes.

Nooooooo! She lets out, laughing.

William stammers.

Sorry.

Er.

It was an accident ...

What an idiot!

Andy puts his wig back in its place, goes into John's bedroom. Looking for his leather jacket among the pile of the other guests' jackets, he discovers John snoozing under layers of coats, jackets and blazers.

John: Andy! What's going on?

Andy: What's going on is that it's time to go to bed.

John: You aren't sleeping here?

Andy: It's over. You'll never see me in this apartment again. The fivesome is over.

Meanwhile, Eddie has started to dance even more intensely. She's acting like someone who's having a great time, but in reality, deep down ...

One day soon, the drugs will destroy her.

4

When John woke up, he didn't know where he was. He gazed at the monochrome ceiling, the photos and drawings hung on the walls, the books and newspapers scattered on either side of the nightstand. He became aware of the dust blanketing the floor, asked himself to whom do these balled-up pants belong. A breeze of fresh air passed over his face. Lifting his head, he discovered a slightly ajar window framing a neither blue nor white sky.

At the end of a long, echoing yawn, he understood he was home. To be more precise, in his own bedroom, in his own bed.

Once up, John indulged in a yoga session, linked to some meditation. Harmony regained, energy restored, he ate, washed up, chose his clothes carefully. Examined the time displayed on his phone's screen. And went back to bed.

John is without a doubt a gifted and promising poet, but first and foremost he is unemployed, unread and unpublished. John also has a problem worth noting: he is incapable of getting up before noon. On top of that, John suffers from a second problem: in the afternoon, his body demands a nap. Still, this second problem wouldn't be anything without problem number three, which can be linked to problem number one, about which many would argue there is no smoke without fire: John ends up completely wasted every night.

If you knew what he'd put in his mouth the day before, you wouldn't expect anything from him the next morning.

Morning: he's almost forgotten to what this word refers. If, by chance, he happens to open his eyes and it's morning, he tells himself there really is no morning. And goes back to sleep. You won't hear anything from him before the start of the afternoon.

If it were up to John, he would only sleep. For that matter, he does practically nothing else. He spends his time drinking, eating and sleeping.

As a result, he has no time to spend on other things. John no longer reads. John no longer attends readings. John doesn't set foot in the Centre for Public Poetry. John receives publication proposals from magazines, poetry associations invite him to give readings in exchange for a fee, meal, drinks, lodging for a night, but he doesn't follow up. Since he went to bed for good, he's stopped writing. Sometimes in the evening a poem comes into his head, but during the night the poem escapes him, and the next morning there is no more poem in his head. In his head, there's only a killer migraine.

John opens his eyes, rubs them with his fist. He moves an arm, breathes, coughs, grunts, scratches his head. He deciphers the time displayed in red characters on the lit-up screen of his blackberry-coloured phone. 2:07 p.m. What is there to do now? John gets up, puts his hands on his waist, yawns, drags his feet over to his kitchenette, makes himself a nice black coffee and drinks it, goes back to lie down on the bed, yawns and yawns again, trying to remember his night.

That night Andy watched John sleep, kept vigil over his friend and, like every morning, got out of bed bright and early.

The telephone rings in John's bedroom.

Normally, John tells Andy about his night. Today, Andy takes the floor.

Andy has his exhibition.

Eleanor is happy to present *The Sleeper*, an exhibition by Andy and John.

The Sleeper has already slept in many different places, in a variety of situations not necessarily the most suited to the practice of sleeping. He has still never slept in an art gallery, on opening night. For him, this is a first. So he arrives very motivated. The artist conceived of a bed that is installed in the space by tossing a mattress on the floor. The man is invited to lie down. He lies down. Everyone waits for him to fall asleep. He falls asleep. He is filmed while he sleeps.

The idea here is to produce a film that begins the moment the man falls asleep and ends when he wakes up. The idea is also for there to be no break between the production of the film and its public presentation. The film is done in one take, which means no cutting, no editing.

Once the Sleeper is up, filming stops and it's time to move on directly to the screening of the film.

The film will be screened at the rate of one showing per day, a single showing. The film's length will determine the hours the venue is open: the exhibition opens, the screening begins, the film ends, the exhibition closes. The exhibition will last for six weeks, including weekends, closed on Tuesdays. The hours of operation will be announced after opening night.

Andy chose to entrust the role of the Sleeper to his friend John. John is a poet, he's currently unemployed, he's also a heavy sleeper. Andy openly says that if he hadn't so often had the opportunity to see John sleeping in any and every circumstance – during a party with loud music, at a table in a restaurant, during a telephone conversation, while waiting for the bus, sitting on the toilet, reading or fucking – it wouldn't have ever occurred to him to make him sleep in an art gallery.

By asking John to embody the Sleeper, Andy is inventing a job that makes the most of his friend's expertise: permanent fatigue, a constant desire to sleep, pleasure while sleeping, the quality of his body at rest. It's delicate work, but it's still work, a little work likely to provide the benefits generally associated with working: the joy of the professional life, a rediscovered self-esteem, a blossoming social life and an improvement in material living conditions.

Andy had a text made for John. His heading: *I'm not sleeping, I'm working*. For the entire duration of the exhibition, it will be available to the public in the form of a double-sided sheet of loose-leaf paper placed at the reception desk.

Luminous rectangles appear on the floors of buildings. It's from these rectangles that the presence of buildings can be discerned. It's from the multiplication of these rectangles that a large city is recognized at night. From a distance, they're points with vague and blurry outlines. Closer, they're lit-up boxes where domestic scenes play out with characters and furniture. One person comes home, exhales, closes her door, removes her shoes, changes clothes, empties her bag, takes out a newspaper, puts the newspaper on the coffee table, turns on the television, mutes the sound, puts on music, opens the window and smokes.

Once night falls, it takes two or three minutes for the streets to light up. While waiting, the public domain is dark, potentially dangerous; this period is unpredictable, thoughts turn bad, incidents lurk, crimes prepare themselves. And then the masses of lights appear. The streetlights bring back the day. Streets, avenues and parks once again become light, legible, happy, safe. Pedestrians leave the shadows for colour, cameras are watching, the front of *M*useum becomes saturated with municipal lighting.

On this opening night, they are all there, guests of the gallery and anonymous opening-goers. They are dressed for the occasion – simply, with discreet elegance. They put more importance on the materials and the cut than on the colours and patterns. A large number of visitors sport glasses that neither correct their vision nor protect them from the sun. They wear glasses with neutral lenses, for the pleasure of wearing glasses that don't standardize sight by correcting it to the nearest tenth. Some people have texts tattooed on their necks. These texts are written in multiple languages – the alphabets themselves vary, such that in order to understand all languages and read all alphabets, you only need to compare these texts. It is very difficult to know how the visitors read and see.

Only five minutes ago the gallery was nearly empty, now all of a sudden everyone is there. The guests came at the same time. All are welcomed by Eleanor. Okay, she's cursing at them, but at least she's talking. Good evening, cocksuckers, welcome, shitheads, why don't you all just go to hell. (She laughs.) Guests and visitors gather around with a glass of something and toot their own horns about topics that more or less deal with the fact that they've ended up at *M*useum on opening night waiting for something to happen. They raise their first glass to their forehead or higher, proclaim to us, and bring the glass to their lips. Then knock it back in one gulp. As of the second glass they are no longer lost in conversation, they go straight to what's important, and what's important here is to drink heavily while chatting in a quality artistic environment.

Eleanor signals for Andy to come mingle with the guests.

Andy approaches, mingles, Eleanor makes introductions.

Do you know Andy?

Until now, only by name.

Sorry, introductions will be for later. Because John appears. What eyes he has – if they can still be called that – red myxomatosis eyes. John's been drinking, so that nothing is different. In fact, this time it was outright encouraged. Tonight the gallery is treating, by virtue of the fact that heavy drinking makes a heavy sleeper.

Gerard and Gerard are in place, meaning each is in a place that can only be his. One adjusts the lighting *a giorno*, the other tends to the camera. The guests finish their drinks, their speeches draw out, words space out, sentences rest in suspense, voices hush. It looks like it's time, it's starting soon.

What were we saying? John heads to the centre of the white room, lies down on the bed, clad in a cotton spandex shirt and pants, and a pair of sneakers with three stripes. He pulls the sheet up around himself, lowers his eyelids, turns over and settles onto his side.

A man falls asleep in a room of *M*useum.

Start of the exhibition.

Come in to this room with its white walls, high ceilings and polished floors.

Back in the old days this room had windows, but when it changed owners, their presence was deemed unnecessary. As a result of the room's new purpose, they were sealed off. People have forgotten that in the old days there were windows. Today the windows are invisible, assimilated by white walls. Yet it's quite possible they will one day resurface.

This room is the object of regular maintenance. It has recently been painted – they must have used an odourless paint because the room doesn't smell like anything. It smells neutral, meaning nothing. You could say that the walls are clean, smooth and shiny, but you should also add that they are bare, white as can be. At the same time, the more you look at them, the more you have reason to think otherwise. And what if the walls were neither all the way white nor completely bare, what if they were a white that hints at being grey? This white-grey would be the result of successive layers of paint, filled-in holes, painted-over inscriptions, traces of what has previously been presented here and covered up in order to move on to the next thing.

The floors are smooth like the pages of a book. Yet they're coarse. Like the pages of a book. The space isn't new, it's been re-new-vated, it's prepared to receive something. It's sometimes white, it's sometimes white-grey. A source of artificial light comes from the ceiling, completed by the specific lighting of the spotlight pointed at the

Sleeper. The room has no shadows. The space is shaped like a cube.

People talk and talk, and during that time the night advances in *M*useum's gallery. At last, it's obvious that the night is progressing to the extent that the guests start to yawn, some leave, others stay. And then very quickly, suddenly, automatically, it's morning.

The guests are sorry, but they really must get going. They would have gladly stayed at the gallery longer, but they have things to do – although they are guests here, other obligations are calling them. They aren't unemployed. They work full-time. They themselves don't even have time to sleep. They aren't poets. These exhibitions with sleeping poets are fine and all, but not everyone has the option to spend his days waiting for a man to wake up. An active life awaits them. After this all-nighter, they go back to the places where they practise their professional activities. They will conduct profitable business while certain others sleep.

Time goes by, converted into time spent sleeping for John, and for the others time spent awake and waiting around. The exhibition follows its course, the hours of sleeping add up according to the fiscal rules that govern the passing time, but in reality no one is really aware of that: they say time is passing and it's passing brusquely. John would be well advised to wake up but that's how it is, he's snoozing – sorry, he's working.

Gerard: What are we deciding? Do we put up a sign with QUIET written in big letters? QUIET, FILMING IN PROGRESS? QUIET, A MAN IS SLEEPING? Or else do we close? DURING THE EXHIBITION, THE GALLERY

IS CLOSED TO THE PUBLIC? Do we shake him? Wake him up?

Eleanor: We don't touch anything. The protocol is very clear: The Sleeper wakes up on his own, at the end of his night of sleeping. The gallery is committed to supporting the poet's sleep. As long as he's sleeping, the gallery stays open. We're open twenty-four hours a day.

Gerard: Sooner or later, John will open his eyes. That's for sure.

Andy: Tomorrow is another day.

The following day is very similar in terms of sleep and cinematographic inactivity. At any rate, it's not exactly the same day as the one before. It's the day after, another day. A new exhibition day is dawning, the second day in the life of the Sleeper. Filming continues.

Andy: This exhibition is a failure, not only is it a failure it's also a disgrace.

The art critics show up, hordes of them coming from all over. Eleanor had no idea so many of them lived in this metropolis, for fucking fuck's sake, how do they reproduce? The art critics enter the gallery, turn toward the welcome desk, they say Hello, Hello, says the receptionist, Thank you for coming, take an info sheet, do you know Andy? 'We'd like to visit the exhibition first.' Very well, then, I'll leave you to take the tour? 'Yes, thank you,' the critics say, walking over to the room with small steps, arms dangling, looking curious, in the manner of art critics at work.

The tour completed, the critics come hang around beside the welcome desk, a place where they are more or less certain to find friends or, in the absence of friends, information. So? attempts the gallerist. 'A must-see,' the critics say. Have a drink, explain, says the gallerist, holding her breath. 'Well on one hand, this guy who isn't waking up, this exhibition, which thwarts expectations, which destroys the artist's desired protocol. No, there's no denying, it's a change, it's different, it makes you wonder, it's interesting. We don't know how things are going to turn out. Which makes for a little suspense. No ... great. But at the same time...' At the same time what? The gallerist quickly exhales. 'At the same time, we aren't sure what to think about it. And by the way, while we're on the subject, what does the artist think about it?'

Call Andy, Eleanor says.

Andy?

Andy!

Andy: I don't know. It's a failure.

Enter the collectors. There are some private collectors, there are some who work for foundations, enterprises, some are there for themselves. Some are recognizable, some have never been seen there before. The gallerist leads the tour. While she emphasizes the unique characteristics of the exhibition with gestures somewhat large and pensive, somewhat short and frank, the collectors keep their hands behind their backs. They say nothing, at least nothing intelligible, they produce grunts only they can understand, collectors' grunts. They play with their eyeglasses, leisurely sliding them along the bridge of their noses, chins lowered, eyes raised, to make the low-angle view favoured for criticizing a piece.

The collectors play with keys at the bottom of their pockets, approve of the gallerist's remarks with a nod, grunt once more, cross and uncross their arms, shake friendly hands, kiss familiar cheeks, raise a hand to address surrounding greetings. Then return to the gallerist's explanations. And that's when they pinch their chins. 'Hm, hm. Yes, yes. I see. Good, good.' Do the collectors like it? 'It's just that...' That what? 'This guy who's sleeping, listen, it sure is beautiful, interesting, original, there's no lack of interest, but think about it for two seconds, how do you want to handle the acquisition of a guy who's sleeping?'

The first visitors arrive. Who is this man? they ask upon discovering the bed occupied by the Sleeper. This man is a living poet. Well, he was a living poet before going to sleep, now it's hard to say. Why is he sleeping? Because he was asked to. Why doesn't he wake up? No one knows. Is he sick? He isn't. Is he in a coma? He isn't. Is he dying? He's in perfect health, he's breathing, his heart's beating. What is he thinking about? What is he dreaming about? Why this withdrawal? Is he still a poet? Is he paid to sleep? We don't know what he's getting out of it, why he's sleeping, what he's thinking about, what he's dreaming about, if he's still into poetry. We only know that his body is there, and indeed he is paid to sleep. To know any more, he would have to get up and tell us.

Andy: I believe John has found a job he likes, a job he has no desire to quit.

In the following weeks, people come to see *The Sleeper* alone or with friends, with or without family, at night for the vigil, in the morning in hopes of witnessing his awakening. They show up at nap time, after, before or between work hours. The visitors stay a while, bring picnics, games for the children, hot or cold drinks for the adults, they bring books and newspapers, or they come with nothing and take a break.

It's not so bad in an art gallery, it feels nice, it smells nice, it's peaceful – take a spot on a bed of cushions, stay as long as you want, no one asks for anything, you can meet people if you want to meet people, time passes, the session is unlimited, nothing happens, a guy is sleeping, it's all out there, no one expects anything else, time goes by, no one sees the time go by.

*T*he *Sleeper*: final days!

In a week, the next opening comes to *M*useum.

Collectors call the gallerist. They announce their great interest in the piece, even if they wish to take some time to think about it. They suggest that the gallerist stay in touch and out of goodwill she urges them to visit *M*useum, so that they can talk specifics. The collectors hang up and seek advice from more informed people: critics, curators, artists, institutional directors. They use all of their capacity for abstraction to visualize the piece among the other pieces in their collections. They call the gallerist again to inform her of their continued consideration.

All of a sudden, a collector is ready to purchase *The Sleeper*.

What? He's buying it as it is, he's buying it now, he's buying it alive, he's ready to bring in a mover at once so they can wrap it and bring it to the stockroom where his private collection sleeps. A collector makes it clear he has money to spend, other collectors do too – they can find nothing better to do than compete with each other, which raises the starting price. But that collector is still ready to pay the highest price. He seems to bestow a lot of importance on *The Sleeper* entering his collection. He's very determined and very well-off.

The time to finalize the sale is now or never. Eleanor and Andy had originally thought about selling the film. But how do you sell a film that's in the process of being filmed?

The exhibition is in its sixth week, the Sleeper is still sleeping, and it is imperative that it be taken down in less than twenty-four hours. In twenty-four hours someone will come to clean and paint a coat of white on the walls. And so begins the hanging of the next exhibition. After thinking about it, Eleanor decides to sell the piece in its state, John in the act of sleeping and being filmed. And Andy, what does he say about it?

Eleanor: Andy hasn't said anything, you know him, we broke the news of our idea to him, he just went hm hm, that's all he was inspired to say, and to us hm means yes, and yes means we sell, so we're selling.

And *The Sleeper* is sold.

RrRrRrRrRrRrRRrR

RrrrrrRrrrrrRrrrrrRrrrrrRrrrr

RrrrrrrrrrffffffffffffffffffffffRrrrrrrrrrrffffffffffffffffff

RrrrrrrrrrruuuuuummmmmmmmmmpfffRrrrrr

Fffffffffffffffffffffffffffffffffff

Cyrille Martinez is a poet and novelist living in Paris. He has performed at public readings in France and abroad on stereotypes of modern language, slang, slogans, jargon and the like. His other novels include *Chansons de france*, *L'enlèvement de Bill Clinton* and *Musique rapide et lente*.

Joseph Patrick Stancil has studied French and translation at UNC-Chapel Hill and New York University. This is his third translation to be published. He lives and works in New York New York.

This book is set in Scotch Modern, a typeface family designed by Nick Shinn in 2008 that embodies the aesthetic and functional qualities of types first appearing during the early 19th century from the hands of Scottish type engravers it was named for. The very first typefaces of this style surfaced around 1810 in Edinburgh from the type foundry Miller & Richard. The style flourished during the Victorian era and maintained its popularity for the 19th and early 20th centuries. These Scotch faces were influenced significantly by the types of Giambatista Bodoni and Firmin Didot, as well as Baskerville's letterforms.

Shinn took his reference from a scientific manual of 1834 that used a ten-point Scotch face for its text. Without using scans, he revived the type by eye on the screen, which resulted in a very true re-creation of the original face.

Printed at the old Coach House on bpNichol Lane in Toronto, Ontario, on Zephyr Antique Laid paper, which was manufactured, acid-free, in Saint-Jérôme, Quebec, from second-growth forests. This book was printed with vegetable-based ink on a 1965 Heidelberg KORD offset litho press. Its pages were folded on a Baumfolder, gathered by hand, bound on a Sulby Auto-Minabinda and trimmed on a Polar single-knife cutter.

Translated by Joseph Patrick Stancil
Edited and designed by Alana Wilcox
Cover by Ingrid Paulson
Photo of Cyrille Martinez by Pauline Abascal
Photo of Joseph Patrick Stancil by Guy Smith

Coach House Books
80 bpNichol Lane
Toronto ON M5S 3J4
Canada

416 979 2217
800 367 6360

mail@chbooks.com
www.chbooks.com